AF669372

# LONGING

## P S Dev

**MINERVA PRESS**
NEW DELHI
ATLANTA LONDON SYDNEY

**LONGING**

Copyright © P S Dev 1999

All Rights Reserved

No part of this book may be reproduced in any form
by photocopying or by any electronic or mechanical means,
including information storage or retrieval systems,
without permission in writing from both the copyright
owner and the publisher of this book.

ISBN 81 7662 041 6

First Published 1999 by
MINERVA PRESS
A1/304 Safdarjung Enclave
New Delhi 110 029

Printed in Great Britain for Minerva Press

# LONGING

*To my dear parents*
*Mrs. and Rev. P. Prasada Rao*
*And*
*Mr. V.S.D., a true friend of our family*

## *About the Author*

P S Dev, a young man of 27 years was a student of Loyala College, Vijayawada, Post-graduated from Andhra University, Visakhapatnam, is at Present a Jr. Lecturer at D.L.B. Jr. College, Visakhapatnam.

His poems appeared in the issues of 'Poet' an International monthly based at Chennai (erstwhile Madras). He also contributes articles to the local newspapers.

# *Acknowledgements*

My brothers Dayanand, Siraj, Sanjay, Joshua and Murali for understanding me and Samy, Bindu and Rana for sparing me their thoughts.

I would like to thank David, Srinivas, Celia, Abijith, P.V.A. Rao and S.V.S.R for their unceasing encouragement throughout my venture. Also, Suzan, Hepsi, Dayana, Ammgar, Finny and John for the joy they gave me.

From the core of my heart I thank Minerva Press, especially Mr. John Brown, for seeing the book through its many stages.

And above all, my dear God, who is more able than able,

Thank you.

# *Preface*

On a railway station destitutes and delinquent children always draw my attention. They witness arriving and departing of trains, passengers of cross cultures with different tongues and varied mannerisms. Frail bodies with shagging limbs, soiled clothes and curious looks. For them the railway station is their home, a place where they can move as they like, and shout and dance in the flickering lights of the platform, overcoming their dark present.

Whenever I see them, my heart yearns to sit with them, to know their past and to know what they feel about the present. But I always restrain myself from doing so 'cos it might bring back sorrow. It once so happened that I had to spend a summer night on a railway station. There, my eyes fell on a pale and frail woman, with a torn saree wrapped around her, eyes swollen out of dropsy, mumps on her neck and lower jaw, injured nose and a cloth bag in hand. I observed her closely with my mind framing thoughts that tried to guess her past and what was in store for her in future. I went up to her, wished her and talked. The novel 'Longing' is a sequential result of my perception of her past.

Of all the characters, Prathiksha is my favourite creation. Though the role she plays is very insignificant but she is the heartbeat of her mother, Katha, who always dreamt of her daughter and longed for goodness in her 'honey'. Prathiksha, incidentally, lived up to the expectations and proved herself to be a good girl before an unknown destitute, who was in fact her own mother.

This book could become a reality only because of Ms Soujanya, whose support to my heart and mind has let this book take its final form. Without her, 'Longing' wouldn't have been a book.

P S Dev

# *Contents*

## *Chapter One*

# Love and Loss

Nature blushed with cheers. People came out of their shelter in relief, as they were much relieved and comforted by a serene rainbow of promises that appeared in the sky. At the outskirts of the town lay a graveyard, a living memory reminding and pinching the people whenever they passed by it. On that ground sat Prathiksha, on a concrete grave built in the memory of a dead soul. She stared deep at her mother's grave and tried to recollect the times she spent with her. Vaguely she remembered, as they were separated by fate as everybody says, but it was an obligatory separation the truth echoes. Prathiksha, who yearned for a meeting with her mother and get the much awaited answers to haunting questions about her father. But they remained unanswered and were buried along with her mother, Kathanjali.

Kathanjali, all through her life cursed and deserted by the society she found was crushed but for fragrance. She was shrewd and smart and was rude to the illegitimate. 'The girl is wise and has a bright future,' wished every young and old. Of her knowledge, many stories were told. 'She looks always as fresh as a daisy,' exclaimed one. 'Oh! She is black yet beautiful,' said another. 'She is kind,' commented one who knew her heart. 'Let her be kind or graceful, honey drops from her lips when she speaks,' twittered all others. Her fragrant childhood faded very soon.

*

She came out of her house, a structure of wood and asbestos sheets, to see her father off who was leaving for his work. He was a labourer who earned bread by his sweat and thus suffered world's fever and fret. She said 'Good bye father. When shall I see you again?'

'Oh darling child! As the sun sets down, I will settle down with you to play,' replied the loving father with a kiss.

She stood at the door till her father made a turn at the way end. She returned to her game on the sand again looking forward to her father's return. She hopped on the ground with a blushing face as she, the loveliest of her flock, traced.

Those were the joyful moments of her life and she relished every moment with mirth and gay.

'Father, why are you so late? We have been waiting for you since one hour.'

'I am sorry, dear girls… ah yea… What shall we ever do?'

The kids settled themselves to their game, chalking out a programme as if they were makers of the world. 'Let's build a temple tower that reaches the sky,' uttered a girl in a satin dress. 'But sky is so high,' reciprocated another. All the four little children indulged themselves in work and couldn't spare their time for others. Their routine-drill, as if the mothers mime. They piled up the sand with their tender palms and thus erected a spectacular form.

'Oh, it's great! We did it,' cheered Katha.

'At last we won it!' exclaimed all others.

'Can we live in it…' Silence reigned supreme and all were in deep thought of the form they wrought.

Suddenly a butterfly fluttered over the tower and sat on it. The beauty of the creature glazed the form.

'Aha! I love it. Let's catch it,' interrupted Rachana. She stood up and stretched her hand towards the butterfly.

'Stop, Rachana, do not disturb it. Let's enjoy the show,' shouted another. As the pandemonium rose, the butterfly flew away.

'Aha...Let's enjoy the show...aha...Let's enjoy the show,' saying this Rachana hopped with joy. Jingling of her anklets and giggling of bangles added beauty to her cute form.

'There's something special about her dimple,' whispered a kid in velvet to another.

All of a sudden, it became cloudy. Birds with drooped feathers settled to their nests and the world seemed to come to rest. Unconscious of this, the kids rose to joy celebrating life as if it was a toy to play with. For them life was indeed a game and the poor girls were not aware of its knife which it shoots into.

The sound of music stood still, everyone stood calm with interrogative looks. They stared at Katha who sat with a dull face. She was not happy. A loud despair surrounded her heart, reflecting the weather, like a lone sparrow with drooped wings.

'Eh, Katha, what happened?'

'What's wrong with you, dear one? Eh! Come on, speak up... What's wrong, dear girl... What happened?'

'Oh! It's drizzling... Let it be... Come speak up, dear.'

All the girls were in a fix. Katha grew sadder moment by moment. Tears rolled down on her blushing cheeks.

'Eh! What happened? Speak up,' pleaded all others. They all circled round her, holding hand in hand, and walked around her, singing:

'Rain, Rain go away,
Come again when we say,
Little Katha wants to play.'

As the storm rose, all rushed to their homes with an unsolved heart. Katha too left for her home, but with a heavy heart. As she reached home, she was surprised to see a huge crowd around her house. 'What happened?' her heart questioned. When she peeped, silence reigned supreme. She could see only a form of flesh and bones lying on the floor. The body was so placid. And she rushed with agony.

Daddy… what… happened… No answer…

*

She spent rest of the days mourning her father's death. She was dropped out of school as her mother confessed that she could not afford her education. Like a bird in cage, she dreamt of freedom, with the cage of confinement around as a heavy burden on her shoulders.

'Katha! Eh Katha… Do you hear me?' With trembling feet she hurried to attend her mother's call.

'Yes, Ma. Did you call me?' seeing Katha, the old lady became furious as if she had seen a bad omen.

'What did you say! Called you… You nasty creature on earth. Are you deaf? I have been shouting since an hour and you didn't respond… What on earth you are up to…' So saying she took an old belt that hung there since her husband's death and came near Katha. Poor lass not knowing what to do shivered with fear. As her fear grew, her mother drew nearer to her, and then the old belt danced on Katha's back. Tears rolled down her cheeks. Tears, the droplets of blood, which gathered out of anguish, strained themselves to flow through her eyes as beads of pain.

Katha's elder sister, Kushala, was a maid of whims and fancies and had a lot of time to fantasise. At seventeen, she had the fullest of her life, a life of mirth and carnal cheer and she thus unfolds her day without strife. Another member of the family was Vishala's brother, who even at thirty does not bother about his livelihood and relies upon his sister for bread and butter. He always whiled away his time with a stray batch of the place all day and it was difficult to trace him. Kushala, the pet of household had many stories untold. The stray girl indulged, always, in carnal whirl with all her frills. She won many hearts with her guile. She was a flirt with smooth flattery as stock in her adventures. 'Her lips were as sweet as honey with diseases many' was the watchword of so many. Yet, many men were led to death of spirit, as she did not know the path of life. This happy-go-lucky lass had a soft corner for Vishala's brother, her maternal uncle who reciprocated the same. Vishala encourages, as it is the desire of her heart.

*

As the light of mortal world slowly settled his body to rest, the cloud was about to cover the world, as its life was a true lie. Katha, who lay on the floor felt uneasy and couldn't sleep. Her toiled body was not able to rest properly and she rolled on the floor, scratching her head, sat up for some time, again, lay down. 'Oh God! What's this? I never felt this uneasiness… Am I OK? I better go to the closet… But how… I have to cross these sleeping stupid… Rather I check it here… Oh, come on, nothing will happen…Everything goes in sleep.' Saying to herself she returned to sleep but to no avail. She cried, 'I cannot suffer… why is my back aching so much. I did not pull anything heavy… Good heavens! My dress… the only dress I have… What to do … What's this unusual happening … What a disgusting thing to happen… I better go and check in the closet.'

Time didn't wait to give her space to sleep. The light of the world rose in cast of the sky, the discovery of strangeness woke her up in shy. Day by day, her toiled body, as the virgin's soil felt the burden of creatures with fading features in sun and shower. She did not have time to look and stare, as there was no one to care and share.

Katha, after her heavy day's work, stood by the moonlight, musing her past. The thought of her friends and good old days with her father filled her eyes with tears…

'Loveliness… I have lost with my loving father… What a lovely sight,' she said to herself as she looked at the neighbour's daughter being cajoled by her mother. She wept and mourned her deprived position, the harshness of her mother, indifference of her sister and crookedness of her uncle… All these thoughts made her sob bitterly. Suddenly, she felt the touch of flesh. Fingers danced on her shoulder as if they were, to translate into her, the tunes of breeze. She turned and was shocked to see a terrible visage with fowl breath. She was scared by the scars of the hand on her shoulder. The hand then reached out to her eyes and wiped away a tear from her cheek.

'Why are you weeping, dear Katha? Eh, Katha. I asked you why do you weep… Oh! Tears are precious do not waste them.' The poor lass was taken aback to hear a melodious note from a wayward crook. 'Katha, Oh, my Katha, answer me… Why do you weep? Look how the place is deserted without your smile… Smile. Oh! Ka-th-an-ja-li… Smile… Aha… Yes, it's great you are smiling now.' As moments passed by the evening filled with the loveliest smiles of Katha.

'Katha. Eh! Katha stupid, what are you doing?' she responded to her mother's call with trembling feet.

'You dirty duckling… How many times I have to call you, eh… yea… You need a good treat…'

'But, Ma… I was talking to…'

'Shut up you alley cat… Don't tell me cock and bull stories.'

'Believe me, Ma… even… you ask him if you wish…'

'Keep your mouth shut, bloody whore…'

Vishala then called her brother and Kushala for supper. She was very much appreciated for the sumptuous meal she served. Perhaps they thought three is a crowd and so didn't invite Katha, who with her swollen eyes, sat sobbing in a corner.

# Chapter Two
# Consummation

The place was quiet and was devoid of human movement as no one could venture out and drown themselves in the scattering sparks of the sun. Oldies recollected their past summer memories and concluded that they had never experienced such heat before. Young men took refugee in A/C cinema halls if they could afford to or tune into multi-channel televisions with their fickle minds. Many teenage girls shared tales of accidental charm and tips of chemical beautification of their skin for a fairer complexion to overcome the dark in their lives. A few studious dames steered their life cautiously as it was prone to get side-tracked by the magnetic power of worldly lust.

The barren road was invaded by a 'kulfi man*'. He was the darling of kids. He rang the bell, halting at every house, reminding children of his arrival. The kulfi bell is music to ears of children and knell to parent's pockets. He passed through every lane of the habitation and was known to everyone. The kulfi man, who was about forty-year-old, had mastered every childish prank and could convince everyone with his playful tricks. He stopped at a house and rang the bell, soliciting his regular customer – Kathanjali.

Kathanjali, who had just entered teens, had become a person of importance for the women in vicinity and a victim to the piercing glances of men and women alike. The

---

* Person who sells Ice creams.

newness in Katha made her virtually a shy person and indifferent to the society.

Responding to the call of kulfi man, Katha opened the door with a watering mouth, and emptied hands off nothingness.

'I am sorry, no one is at home,' said Katha.

'So what?' answered the kulfi man.

'I don't have money to buy a kulfi.'

'You take it. I will recover it afterwards.'

'No, I can't. Mother scolds me.'

'Hey, PaPa*. No problem. You have the kulfi and don't think of money. I know how to handle your mother.'

'Oh, you always say like this. But I faced the consequences last week. Didn't you tell me the same and convinced me to have a kulfi on credit? Later when Mother came to know…' tears rolled down her cheeks as she spoke, '…she beat me. And so, I am sorry uncle, I don't want to have another such experience… She never says anything in front of you. But after you go… the old belt of my father dances on my back.'

Katha's unmindful confession broke as she observed glaring looks of the kulfi man, which made a laser study of her anatomy. She was confused at the bemused kulfi man who was holding a melting kulfi, yet afraid of his ogling gaze, ran inside and slammed the doors. She was very tense and lay on the floor. Such curious glances haunted her every moment and she was unable to understand the sudden attitudinal change in the kulfi man.

'He had always been so sweet to me and played many games too. Many a time I thanked God for his company in my heart, for he is the only outsider whom I can speak to at ease in front of my house everyday. Our daily meetings would become a sweet memory till the next happened. But

---

* Young girl.

today… he behaved like this… I cannot understand… not only he… I have observed many looking at me as if I am a foreigner… Oh! Leave alone others, I have found the same in my sister's attitude. She observes every inch of my body… never looks into my eyes…and… that grandpa who sells milk… this morning he did not turn his eyes away which fell on my chest, and gave a toothless smile. An Aunty in neighbour whispered something to her friends looking at my hips, and giggled among themselves… Yesterday, mama*, who made me sit on his lap as soon as he got back all through yesteryears, threw looks of different kind, patted my buttocks whenever and wherever opportunity shot in… Adding to all these bloody people… shit… that sudden discharge… Oh, my God… You created a discomfort… OK… but why the pain… what did I do… I can't concentrate… I always feel so dizzy… not one or two hours… but five days of discomfort… ah… ah… ah… This bloody shitful process had become a humour in that cinema which I had watched on a neighbour's television… People had a hearty laugh at it, as if it was a healthy joke played on sick people. Filthy people… filthy movies…' Thus Katha bewildered at the strangeness of the age-old society she dwelled in.

Suddenly, she was reminded of the cooking job for the evening meal. She wanted to refresh herself with a cold bath and prepared everything she needed for it. She stood bare wondering at the growth on her body, praising her cute form with a proud feeling. As her hands danced on every mould and curve she was amazed at the architectural expertise of the Creator.

The sudden thought of entanglement in lustful glances pierced her mind and she cursed her beautiful form as it turned out to be a nightmare for her. As she was alone, she had made the time useful for her. She remembered people

---

* Maternal uncle.

commenting on her dark complexion with ugliness. When she looked into the mirror she found something arresting in her. A charm that drew her own attention. Her conclusion on her beauty was overtaken by the insane comments of unaesthetic minds. Her silent query was halted with a thought. She wore her torn petticoat, covered her bosom with a cotton towel, stepped out and plucked few hibiscus from the garden, mixed turmeric in oil and rubbed it all over her body. She took half an hour to finish the job and make herself sure what she did was complete. She applied turmeric thrice on her face and laughed at the golden hue on her. She smiled pitifully at herself as she was taken back at the unwanted hair on her arms. She fell into a dilemma and rubbed the turmeric paste on the part of unwanted hair till she felt the pain. When she felt the job was perfect, she frolicked around to the blaring tunes coming from the street behind.

She finished her bath and hesitated to wear that worn-out petticoat and fasten her grown-up organs. It was stinking but she could not help it. All the fresh ones belonged to her sister and she could not have one. She thought of discarding it for the night and wore her one of sister's thrown away skirt, wearing nothing underneath.

*

Vishala and Kushala returned home with a luggage of clothes, food stuff and pleasantries but nothing to share with her. She didn't mind as she was used to it. Vishala was very happy and dreaming to take on a long pilgrimage. Kushala tried on her new pair of dress they had bought and looked into the mirror. She set her dress and posture to look and feel more attractive, set loose her hair, covered her make-believe bosom with it, which was actually flattened and unappetising. She moved around Katha, in vain, trying to plant a seed of jealousy in her. Then she went beside her uncle and shared pleasantries with him.

Kathanjali had her supper after washing the utensils and setting them. She lay on the floor while the rest slept in the backyard to feel the fresh breeze. She went into a deep sleep, as she was tired of day's work and mental agony.

The man in the house, Vishala's brother suffered from sleeplessness as he was haunted by an unfulfilled desire, a desire quite normal, and which ripens in haste but subsides by lovemaking or lust making. He got up from the cot, strolled in the backyard, lighted a cigar, sipped some leftover arrack, jogged on the road, and tried all the ways to subside it. After sometime, he went in to have a glass of water to quench his thirst. As he looked at Kathanjali sleeping he grew more thirsty and resolved to have the nectar by emitting his own. He paced a few steps ahead and lay beside her, stroking her hair. Katha felt disturbed for a while but drowsed herself into the sleep. He caressed her large eyes and kissed them. His fingers danced on Katha's delicate jaw and smothered the rose lips. He led his index finger through her lips and played on her shining teeth, while his forearm rested on firm and symmetrical breasts of Kathanjali.

Disturbed Katha woke up in confusion and was bemused at her Mama's behaviour.

'Mama, what are you doing here?' inquired Katha.

'Uh… Katha, how are you feeling now?' he questioned.

'Feeling what? I am OK. Were you not sleeping all this time?'

'No, dear one, I am thirsty… I would like to quench it.'

'Oh! Why can't you fetch it yourself… for this you had to wake me up?'

'I thought of it at start… but I disturbed you intentionally.'

'Oh, Mama… you are very shrewd,' so saying she got up to fetch him water. The cloth string of her skirt, which he was holding, unfastened as she stood up. She was puzzled at the incident and slammed on the floor with shyness, while the animal in him rose to the occasion and invaded the virgin soul. She felt the humid perspiration of the unwanted guest at an unprepared time. While he bruised her and squeezed her, her sandwiched breasts felt the weight of the sulphurous beast and her unblemished buttocks were flattened. She resisted him with all her energy but surrendered by the indifferent attitude of her family.

His desire fulfilled
While her body bled.

The day broke. No one found change in either the weather or the scenic set up of nature. Kathanjali, with tearful swollen eyes, felt the change through the experience of her captured virginity. She didn't find anything lost in the physical form. After all, blood sheds whenever the body is ruptured or injured or wounded. She didn't feel the loss between the thighs or in the painfully squeezed breasts but between the ears, something disturbing, something vacant, something like blissful innocence was taken away, something like lush beautiful lawn was plundered by buffalo hoofs, that became a nightmare in every movement at every moment.

Nature quite natural
In its beauty splendour
Showers of rain and blazing Sun
Chirping of crickets and melody of cuckoo
Tail wagging dog and run away cat
Holy tulsi and delicacy of mustard
Blooming rose and fading jasmine
Formation of algae and pace of a snail
All remained the same
But the amusement of yesteryears

Found no place now
In the mind of this dame.

*

Kushala was plucking jasmines in the backyard and Vishala was chatting with knowledgeable ignorant neighbours regarding disposing of their daughters. Each submitted to the other a white paper of possessions with which they could purchase a well-to-do gentleman to save their name and fame and free themselves of their daughters. They shared their idea of husbands-to-be for their daughters – small, fair, muscular, earning a lot, should have large bucks of parent's property, but not parents, preferably the only son. They are quite rational for flesh and bones, built body taking to the altar of riches, garlanding with currency notes and adorned with iron and steel machines to be at their beck and call. What else does a girl need? Thus they had pondered over the idea of a husband-to-be, who gave a ring or tie a sacred thread around the neck to take the girl away.

Kathanjali, who was over-hearing, questioned herself. 'Is that what a marriage is? Is it not anything more than that… maybe… 'Cos Mom and Aunt were married all these years and they were giving out what they feel about it, so marriage can be bought.' Katha thought and she was puzzled at the thought of the oldies, as they were limited only to the extent of purchasing a marriage, but not thinking of the 'resale value'. She suddenly recollected her distant cousin dabbling over depreciation account for his board exams. 'Perhaps I shall ask him.' Aha. She smiled in her mind.

*

Vishala's brother entered in a hurried steps and inquired Kushala about Kathanjali, 'Why do you want her?' Kushala questioned him.

'No, no… I just want to know, where is she… what work can I have with her… my love… my only love.' So saying he hugged and kissed her.

Kushala, who was very anxious of his plans for finding a job, revealed all her worry to him.

'Kushala… I want to leave this place and go to a distant place to earn my bread… I long to be away so that I may not be hooked…'

'What?' interrupted Kushala.

'I mean… I don't want to be in this place forever and be a burden...' he raised his voice that his sister should hear, 'to my sister and to you… you marrying an unemployed husband…'

'What… what did you say?' Vishala shot herself into the conversation. 'You wait a month, we will go together, and stay there till you get the job… mark… that filthy duckling should not know of it… She will stay here alone living on that stuff in the sack till we get back…'

'What if she asks us… OK… not she… others?' asked Kushala.

'We are going on a pilgrimage,' brother and sister together burst out laughing.

Kushala and her uncle stared each other blindfolded of the surrounding.

*

'Katha…eh! Kathanjali, would you like to marry me?' he asked her.

'What… oh… but I got nothing to buy you with?' murmured Kathanjali.

'Ah… what did you say? You got nothing to buy me… what do you mean?'

'I mean what I say… what is marriage… buying a man in cash or kind… Don't pierce me with your looks… That is what Mom and Aunt discussed over.'

'Marriage is something… something great… it involves not only money… living together… togetherness makes a marriage.'

'Togetherness means a crowd… I mean… you mean the togetherness with sister… with me and I don't know of the others, of course.'

'Oh! I swear Kathanjali… if I say anything I mean it with you only…'

'As the sun sets… your philosophy of togetherness rises in your heart… You feel happy in the company of my sister… Of course the day approves of it… you crave for the togetherness with me in the cover of darkness… I told you many times that I am not satisfied with what you call an eternal bond… rather I feel that I am chained with guilty,' confessed Katha.

'Ah… I have a remedy for it… You think that I am after your money… what do you have to buy me… nothing… still I am after you… You say that I behave in the same way with Kushala… Yes… I have to… otherwise I can't have my bread and shelter… you call me a hypocrite… but unless I play a double game… my survival is at stake… not only mine… yours too… OK… dear girl… to make you believe me… I'll marry you.' So saying he tied a thread around her neck and said that they were married. Katha, bewildered at his behaviour, questioned him the authorisation of marriage. He laughed at her philosophical enquiry and told her that the thread was sanctified by the chief priest of the temple. He tried to convince her that if the thread is around one's neck that person is deemed to be married.

Katha was puzzled at the situation and at his authorisation of marriage by a common ritual with a complex meaning. She did not want the issue to be complicated. She told him, 'Mama, I cannot accept a marriage by this common ritual. I wish to know whether the ritual you performed is a manifestation of bond cemented with love... acceptance of your heart to take me as I am... assertion to share all my woes and sorrows cos I may not give joys... Vow to bear the stink of my sweat and foul breath of my uncleaned mouth... For your word togetherness is not only to be remained in the envelope of night hereafter but all through the day and night together.'

He was shocked at the logical mind of Kathanjali at first, but he settled the matter with his serpentine wiles saying that he loved her and the love sprang form the depth of his heart. He swore that he would never leave her in his life, saying this he took her into his arms that led themselves to feel the bliss of eternal bond, as he called it.

Katha was the most satiated being for she felt neither injured nor wounded as she used to feel before whenever the same act took place. She felt all those times that the act was acted upon her and she never took part in it 'cos she never wished to at that time.

Katha was joyous at the blissful union they experienced while he was relaxing from the tiresome work he accomplished. She dreamt of her happy married life while he cursed himself for his hasty act of so-called marriage to fulfil an act that lasted for a moment.

Their parted thoughts together halted as Kushala and Vishala returned from a close relative who was staying in a distant area. He rose and hurriedly took away the sacred thread around Katha's neck, smiled at his sister and cracked a joke on Kushala, the dame of his heart. Kushala, who held him in her hand, took him out and asked Kathanjali for a cup of tea. He followed her into the backyard pouring out all his love and affection.

*

In the evening, he accompanied Kathanjali to a General Stores and made a confession of logical reasoning. He told her that their marriage should be kept a secret for both their lives' sake. He would go to a distant land to make a living on his own and then he would take her as his wife in the company of guests to witness the marriage.

'Are you sure of it?' Katha questioned.

'Oh! Katha you always suspect me as your father did... You never believe me. I married you with the ritual of holy thread...'

'...And you took it off.' Katha interrupted.

'Oh! Katha... I took it off for your sake... your mother and sister are indifferent to you and they never like you and you know all that... they may go to any extent to harass you... that is why I did like that,' he tried to convince her.

'OK, Mama. Whatever it may be... you are my husband and I rely on you. You... I will wait for you to return as a successful man... you know I don't believe in this ritual... marriage is a bond of love and a perfect understanding of hearts... one should be ready to bear with the faults then eager to share the joys and pleasantries. Marriage is forever a matter of understanding and not a matter of convenience for a moment,' saying she kissed him in the darkness in light of hope for life to be enjoyed and cherished.

*

Kushala opened the door in response to the call bell and was astonished to see a police constable with his furious looks asking for her maternal uncle. She couldn't respond immediately as his grim face indicated a very gravesome incident took place and her place and her uncle was part of it. She knew her uncle pretty well and his foul pursuits which always received complaints from the people around – petty thefts, eve teasing, assaulting others in influence of alcohol etc., but it never went to notice of the police.

Police constable was very angry at her irresponsible silence and yelled at her. 'Where is he… eh… how is he related to you… come on… answer me…' Vishala, who was not aware of the unwelcome guest hurried to the entrance door. She was taken aback to look at the constable and was tensed at the situation. After she came to know that he came for her brother, she tried to pacify the situation requesting the unwelcome guest to cover it very shrewdly. She welcomed him into the house and inquired him would he preferred coffee or tea. She asked him to take seat, while she switched on the fan. She asked Kushala to offer tea and snack to the 'inspector'. The very 'inspector' sounded melodious to the much-awaiting constable and was pleased with the royal treatment he was receiving at the culprit's residence. They exchanged pleasantries forgetting the unpleasant act her brother committed.

Suddenly the constable beheld the unfaded charisma of Vishala. While she took hold of the situation and questioned inspector for his arrival. And he gave a brief account of the crime. 'He tried to stab a man as he refused to give money and he was caught, now he is in jail but we can release him anyway.' Vishala agreed for the same and saw the constable off. Constable left with a gratitude for the hospitality and a promise to visit again.

The uncle was released from the police station in exchange of few currency notes as a token of gratitude.

*

Kathanjali was sipping coffee when an old friend of hers, Rachana and her sister visited the household. Katha loved all and she was loved by all. Rachana's sister found some change in her, a feeling of discomfort on her face. She inquired whether she was bothered by any problem. The very inquiry regarding her health made Kathanjali fly with joy. The question about her discomfort made her feel more comfortable than ever, as sometimes soft words may heal a cancerous wound.

Kathanjali complained that she was feeling dizzy and uneasy, a feeling of strangeness enveloped her mind. She could not come out of it, physiological change influenced her mind to such extent that she could not concentrate on her routine work and thus faced music from her mother. That they found the consequence of lovemaking with her uncle, her husband of course, made all the difference. The unwanted guest on that dreadful night, later accepted in heart to be one with her, and left a lasting impact she never dreamt of. Wanted things, however painful they are, give pleasure. Unwanted things, however pleasant they are, remain but as beads of pain.

The self diagnosis that she was going to be a mother made her mirthful at first, but that feeling of ecstasy slowly degraded to be a painful shame by logical reasoning. She was never married by her will, her husband was not sure of himself. Endurance of the physical plain together with mental strain, because of the unconcealed truth, made her day by day a living dead being.

Kushala, Vishala and her brother made all arrangements to leave for a distant land where he could find work. Vishala asked Katha to take care of the house and to live on the stuff they left. They bade farewell to all near and dear ones saying that they were going on a pilgrimage.

Kathanjali called her husband. In fact she tried many times, to meet him. She revealed to him her situation. With an astonished face he remained silent but hurriedly left the place responding to his sister's call, who was waiting with the luggage on the road.

# Chapter Three
# Labour

Katha was alone loitering in the house, dreaming of her motherhood. What to name the child… how to bring her up… All these questions she asked herself made her mind entangle in a state of confusion. Suddenly, a knock on the door knocked her mind to remind her state.

'Where is Vishala?'

'Ma isn't here.'

'Kushala?'

'No one's at home. Everyone left for hell…' Katha held her tongue back.

'What… what did you say?'

'Oh! That is Ma, Kushala left to say hello.'

'What happened to you today?' so saying, the visitor left the place.

Katha, relieved of the conversation, closed the door, then lay on the wooden cot, enjoying every moment and movement of freedom in the house. Never did she lie on the cot and her body knew no comfort since her father's death. Vishala's pilgrimage gave her a change to heal her wounded body and injured heart, for every beat of her heart she pondered of death. Her very imagination gave her refuge in every speculation of life's doubt. Her very relationship with her uncle, his promise of return, her marriage in secret, their consummation at a hiding place, her sister's infatuation for the one she was married to, neighbour's whispers about her life, many times unsettled peace and made her many times to end it as a fantasy, the child in her womb, the rushing of her blood in her veins, the beat of the heart for child, longing for her husband, mourning of her father's death. 'Is it all fantasy' or 'the fantasy of life'. She mused a while to endure life's strife, the double-edged knife. While she was in deep thought, the itch in her body pricked her, followed by a gush of life's fluid that made its way out. Pain reached its zenith. She cried in ecstasy, a longing for her love child. Her body wrinkled. Movement of legs was rapid. A sound of her heart. She could not call out for help as no one was around. She paced in heavy steps to the door, tried to open it, but in vain. Her faltering position could not withstand. She fell on the floor and yelled in pain for help that was reciprocated by her grand aunt who stayed nearby. They made way to the nearby Govt. hospital.

She lay on the stretcher. Labour is laborious. She cried for the God above and pleaded to the nurse below. All the strain lasted for few hours, a pain that her life never expected covers. She cried as much as her nerves allowed her to, the very cry of pain followed by a cry of a new-born girl.

*

'Oh! She is cute, commented nurse. Katha, a mother now, said nothing, but shed tears at the fruit of her own seed, a fulfilled dream of her heart. She spent her time in hospital in days of fulfilment. To disturb her celebration, a nurse strolled in with a message, which pierced through her ears as a curse.

'Katha, you are supposed to be discharged now. Are you ready?'

'Where?'

'No, Katha, you are all right now. Your baby is healthy and she is your wealth.'

'But, sister… where… where do I go? OK… When shall I leave?'

'Kathanjali, I understand your position. You are being deserted, that's what you feel… you are not alone dear girl – you got your child with you. In her joy you can endure the suffering.'

Katha, not knowing what to say, sobbed in grief and said, 'Thank you, dear sister… I owe you a lot… only gratitude to you all through in my life…I cannot repay you your love for me, dear sister. Thank you very much. Thanks a lot.' As the words poured from her trembling lips, tears rolled down the blushing cheeks.

Looking at Katha, nurse's eyes became wet but she tried to control her emotions, restraining tears in all her fear. She hugged Katha and kissed her.

'Oh, Katha… why are you weeping?' Looking at that sweet babe she said, 'Aha look at her wide wild eyes… So beautiful is she.'

'But she is a bit dark,' interrupted Katha.

'So what… she is… What do you want to call her…' asked the nurse.

'You mean the name for her. Yes, what should I name her? She is the delight of my eyes… who made me forget all my sorrow… the time I conceived her is the twilight of my life… with her birth I am able to wish good marrow to life… What shall I call her, dear sister, tell me what shall I?'

'Your daughter, your wish,' said the nurse, nursing the baby.

'Yes… I have an idea… I conceived her of nothingness of heart, got nothing to call my own, every movement at every moment of her drove me to introspection, as the time drew nearer I was able to forget everything and she became the sweetest of my heart.' The nurse left as she was called by the doctor. Katha turned back wandering in a to and fro situation. 'Where shall I go… Who will look after me… Oh, Aunty is there. Let's endure the suffering for sometime. I'll write to her father… but address… what to do… I'll find out somehow or the other and inform him of his cute child. I know he will rush in a moment. Yes I know… I suppose he would be dreaming of his daughter. Six months rolled on. He promised me that he would return in a few days… He deceived me… No… Never. He was never a person of that kind… why didn't he at least drop a word through someone… Isn't he a person with a heart… No, he is a cheat… He cheated me with his sweet sounding promises. I remembered promises are never kept… attempted… for the sake of his grown up droplet seed he may return… Yes he will… but how to convey… I am handicapped… I can't do anything… can't do anything…'

Katha sat on an iron chair. Tears, which sprang from her mournful heart, rolled on her cheek and fell on the child in deep shimmer. The bitter teardrop gave a cold kiss to the infant who woke up with a cry. She set herself to feed the baby, a time that was pleasant for her. 'Thank God in heaven above for He is gracious enough to grant me the privilege of satisfying my daughter's hunger as she affords something.' While nursing her baby she had a glance at the shabby look of her pale and lean image in mirror fixed to the wall. 'Oh how I wish that it is a writing on the wall so as to say that I am on verge of death. Death, the eternal sleep, undistributed rest a state of forgetfulness, a canopy of blissful estate where none had power to dictate terms… a marriage of no entanglements… Oh yes… when shall I attain that blissful state.' So musing, her hands felt soft touch of the sweet babe wrapped in cotton wool. The very touch of the flesh touched her heart and made her breathless for a moment. The dreadful moments of blissful estate soon faded with a realisation of her motherhood, a bond attachment of being inseparable guided by its polestar love, the word with which one calls that relationship, a word expressed in action to make itself understandable rather than in sweet sounding phrases. Katha looked at her daughter deeply and found that the little girl was not bothered of her position. Smile a while, cry a while and sleep a while. This makes the world of the child who is not touched with the fever and fret of her mom's world. 'I envy you, darling,' saying Katha kissed her infant lass and thought of arranging for splash.

'Kathanjali, can I come in?'

'Yes.'

'Are you ready to vacate the room because someone wants to rush into.'

'But Madam, I am waiting for my grand aunt. Soon after she comes, I will leave the place.'

'Grand aunt… of yours… what about your husband?'

'He is away on his job. My mother and sister also…'

'Stop nonsense… enough of your stories… who is going to pay the bill then?'

'Don't be angry, Madam. I'll fetch it somehow.'

'Fetch? What do you think of yourself?'

'No… Yes… I mean, my aunt is going to bring the amount. Now OK.'

As the angry manager of the hospital pondered over the situation of Katha, the nurse who loved Katha stepped in and wished the madam in all her obedience.

'Sister… Talk to this girl once… she says that she has no one to look after her, save… who's that… grand aunt.'

'I know, Madam. She is almost deserted. Don't worry about the expenses. I have resolved to accept the burden.'

'Oh no… money doesn't matter… I am just curious… I am not… you know… I am not at all bothered about money.' So saying, the manager made an exit.

Katha, not knowing what to do, submerged herself in tears. 'Katha… Katha, do not worry, accept the reality… this is one of the lessons… accept that you have no one… I am here… I am here… I am your sister… I'll take care of you. OK. Smile, dear girl.' Confronted by the nurse, Katha mused a while of her situation. The only person she loved much in life was her father. He was no more. The person she believed in is a dilemma of betrayal. She decided in her mind that she was born alone into the world. She glanced at her daughter and thought, 'Yes… she is here since five days. She knows me and the nurse who cleans up the room daily. She is not aware of her father, grand mother or any else in the world. Relations are thus formed… if she grows up here the inmates of the place are her relatives, loved ones, hearts' favourites and so on. I am alone here safe in the company of my daughter and the affectionate nurse, I alone have to endure life's suffering... looking for someone to share with me and care for me in a sweet dream… Yes. I'll fight till the end of my life.' So resolved, Katha packed up all the things in the hospital in a moment, the very tiny luggage of things amused her and said to herself, 'Travel light.' 'Travel light!' repeated the nurse, who stepped in. 'Yes, sister. Travel light. We have to endure life's long journey.

Travel long
Travel light
Travel with a smile
Travel many a mile.

'Oh! Katha, poetic. Lot of change in you. You are positive. I love it… Aha… Where are you heading? Your grand aunt didn't turn up. Where do you want to go?'

'No grand aunt… no nothing… I am going to make grand adventure,' saying so, Kathanjali took her little daughter in her arms, picked up her luggage and made an exit looking forward.

*

The world outside seemed to be very strange as she strolled. She felt herself as if she was on a pilgrimage to wash away all her sins, a sack shoulder bag and a baby wrapped around with cotton roses, and she in a torn off dress. All this seemed to the onlooker as a castaway girl. The very appearance of her draws pity. And hurried steps in her movement rise suspicion and wonder looks around the place. She is explaining resemblance of arms carrying infant and pale cheeks, and the beat of her heart conveyed her that she is lonely in the crowd. Yet she awaited pity and kindness from around. But who cares.

Life
So entangled
With cares and worries
It's hard to find
One to share and care

As she moved a little further, she came under the shade of a tree that made her feel as if her tiredness was faded in a whiff. 'How pleasant it is to sit here… I feel as if I am relieved of all my burden… I feel that I am being confronted… How the birds live in happiness… They build their nests and go on their job, leaving their babies and return… Look how that bird is feeding… yea… it's so pleasant to feed a child… When birds, such tiny creatures live in such a harmony, why do we people fight against one another? There are many things to be learnt from birds… We live in the same nest in one's own world… so we never share or care like those birds… eye… in pure… Oh, who is the woman… she is neither old nor weak, is carrying a stick… perhaps a protective measure… She comes near me… Her eyes are so red… she is tired… why she stares at me as if I have intruded into her world… let's ask her…'

'Who are you?' asked Katha.

'That's what I have to ask you!' countered the woman.

'I am on a pilgrimage… I sat here to relieve myself of my weariness. It seems you are also tired… relax for sometime. This tree has a magic of relief.'

'Oh! That I discovered a long time back.'

'I thought you are a tramp as I am… How long have you been here?'

'I don't know… I don't remember… Time just rolled on… you know I never count time by days but by experiences.'

'Oh great! You speak philosophy.'

'You will too, if you stay here for few days.'

'Is the place so great?'

'Of course! You yourself spoke of 'magical relief' a few moments ago?'

'Ah yes. I really felt that the comfort, which I never expected, was offered to me by the tree.'

'Not only to you, many took shelter under this tree.'

'No I am not talking of shelter, but of the way I am soothed by this great tree.'

'Where do you go for alms?'

'What… alms? What do you think I am?'

'I think of you as you are.'

'Do I look like a beggar?'

'Beggars are not foreigners! You can't make out a beggar by his looks.'

'OK, enough of you. Why did you call me a beggar?'

'Where did you get that child?'

'Oh! Stop it. This child is my daughter to whom I gave her birth a days back.'

'Oh! There is a kind of begging with infant in arms to draw sympathy… I thought of you a case of this kind.'

'Are you a deserted woman?'

'Deserted… I walked away from life to start afresh,' saying Katha revealed all twists and turns of her life.

'Anyway, what's your name,' asked Katha.

'I never remember of people calling me.'

'Don't you have a name of your own?'

'How can I when no one calls me by my name?'

'Why, people never called you?'

'They call me with the names I dislike.'

'Like what?'

'Sometimes alley cat, dirty whore…'

'Hey, who is she… my goodness she is coming near… Oh my God!'

'Don't worry Katha. She is not mad, as you think or bad either. She is like us who take refuge under this tree.'

'…But her hair, weakling figure, torn clothes all seems to me as crazy woman.'

'Ah. She is not crazy, the people, well dressed going in suits are crazy… look at her injured back… she was almost stoned to death last week.'

'How come?'

'She was on her usual walk in the evening. Her hungry stomach glanced leftovers behind a function hall… look at that blue building… there on the left side… she hurried there to grab some to fill her stomach… Poor lass… she didn't do anything… She just bent down to take… all of a sudden she heard a scream of a boy of ten... She turned back in quick pace... you see, that bloody babu thought that she frightened him… thus took his child and threw stones at her back… my God… she almost fainted.'

'Oh, Good Heavens! Is the world so rough?'

'Yeah… of course… as long as you are not tough.'

'I hate the way you talk…'

'And you hate the way I live, Katha…'

'No nothing like that… look… she stares at me… I am a bit afraid of her…'

'That's the way of the world. Yeah, dear Katha, people judge by outward appearance.'

'Enough of you. She is coming near me.'

'Oh! Come on... She is not only a woman with flesh, blood and bones, she has a heart too.'

'OK... OK... What do I call her?'

As both were conversing, the shabby woman reflecting her marsh present approached them on limping foot. Her robe is enough to cover the nakedness of her nude truth, eyes as red as burning charcoal, wrinkled cheeks increased her age, shaggy limbs, soiled body exhausts the stink of world's gutter. She giggled as she glanced at Katha, stretched her hand for a warm handshake with Katha. Katha, who was frightened at her ridiculous look, her cold heart warmed up with affection and admiration at the angel in guise of a crook.

'Eh... Who is she?'

'She is Katha... Kathanjali.'

'Oh shut up. I didn't enquire about the damn bloody name.'

'Oh no! It's such a sweet name.'

'Enough of your pranks, stupid whore. I want to know who the bloody female is she?'

'She...'

'Oh you keep your stinking mouth shut. You answer me. Who are you?' Katha was happy at the warm mannerism at first, but was taken aback with a sudden change of furiousness for which she is more afraid, worse at the behaviour of the mad woman. The woman was very much angry at the dumb behaviour of Katha. 'Yes? Who are you? Where are you from? Why did you come here? ...Speak up, you stupid alley cat.'

'Shut up. I am not an alley cat. What do you think I am?' Katha burst out with the response, as she was startled with the comment.

'What can I think unless you reveal yourself?'

'I am on a pilgrimage... and she is my daughter.'

'Pilgrimage... aha... pilgrimage... Eh... Look she is on a pilgrimage... pilgrimage to wash her sins... aha... I am interested. Tell me why are you on a pilgrimage, eh?'

'Don't bother her with your questions. It seems she hasn't had anything to eat. Let's give her something, first.'

'I got something which I picked up from the streets, but will she accept that?'

'Oh! You first offer her.'

'No, no, no. Don't misunderstand me. I am just pondering whether she will accept it or not, for I picked it up from the street while someone threw it away. It is a street just by the pissing alley.'

'Where else do we pick up from everyday?'

'You didn't get me, bloody nut. She says she is not an alley cat. So how can she eat food picked up by the pissing alley?'

'Oh! Stop that nonsense,' Katha interrupted. 'I am very much thankful for your hospitalities but I am not in mood to eat anything. So better stop talking of food, where you got it from or decide who is an alley cat or a gutter pig.'

'OK, Katha. We are not bothered whether you are hungry or not, we will keep your share. You have it whenever you feel like.'

'Oh, no think about me. Have the full amount. Moreover my stomach is filled up with description of the kind of food you brought.'

The two staring women had their meal to their stomach full, while Prathiksha cried with hunger. Large-hearted little Prathiksha didn't know the disgusted place she is dwelling in, could not feel the stink of the gutter which passes by them, nor felt uncomfortable in the company of shabby women. She is true to herself and to the world. She is hungry and she is communicating.

When Katha fed her little daughter and put her to sleep, she was satisfied and her heart started beating faster in symphony with the thundersome weather. Place around her slowly covered with darkness and her gloomy mind interrogating itself of the shelter for her darling daughter. Clouds swelled up with burden of life's vapour wished to empty themselves with a light drizzle. She mused awhile of her condition, amidst the labyrinth crowd on the Highway she felt of herself as a lonely person in the crowd. The rush of buzzing creatures for stomach's sake appeared so inferior to the free morning, birds above and stray animals below. She looked up at the sky so spacious and dark, calm and placid as a dead man's visage. The people below on Earth thronged together running for shelter as a herd of stags frightened of the jungle king.

Kathanjali's surprise thoughts came to a halt as she felt the drop of rain on the cheek, which knocked her to conscience and hurried to her daughter. Prathiksha, unaware of all things happening, sleeping undisturbed, seemed as an angel pondering over the stinking world.

Katha, holding her daughter in her arms, looked around for the two companions of her under the tree. She couldn't trace them and she tried to call, but how to call passed the question.

'Oh, yes. Filthy duckling,' she shouted to the heights for those two women but of no use. Suddenly drizzle turned to a tornado. Katha looked for shelter and at last she traced an old building where people crowded for the same. She hurried in hasty steps to the building, forced herself in, set Prathiksha in a cosy corner and prayed to God. She denounced herself for praying to God as she is keeping faith in the existence of God. 'God is good only for great people. God is greatness,' said to herself, felt bad with repentance, looking at the lame beggar praising God for more alms in his bowl. He increased his sound, trying to draw attention of all gathered there. Katha, looking at the drama happening, thought:

Nothing is spared
For advertisement
Nothing is less
To take advantage
Nothing is more
For one's height
Nothing is cheap
To keep purse intact
In the name of great
Something happens
In the name of small
Nothing happens
In the name of God
Everything happens
Nothing is spared
In advertisement
If God is spared
Everything is lost
Advertise the God
Nothing you lose.

Her pondering heart disturbed with a cry of Prathiksha, was astonished at the deserted place she was in. No one was around, save that lunatic woman and other companions under the tree. The place was quiet, reflecting the twilight time.

'Hey, I looked for you. When did you come?'

'We made our way long time back. This place, you know, is a temple for us… a hopeful refuge in chill and shower.' Katha was bewildered at the philosophical notes from the old woman. 'From where had she gained the knowledge?' she questioned herself. 'Life is but a ceremonial toy for this woman.' Prathiksha, who was hungry and annoyed, gave a loud cry. Cry was perhaps the communicative device of a human being. Katha cajoled her daughter and said to herself something unusual.

The delight of my heart
You feast me with thine wild eyes
Poor am I to pay you a price.

Her heart was wounded for she could not even spare a piece of cloth for her daughter. A feeling so harsh humiliated her ego. Can't but take the situation for granted. She shared the same with her companion and in response, the woman smiled and hummed a verse of her childhood.

God is truth; Truth is naked
'Shame,' they said for they love façade
God felt the shame, turned dumb and lame
Senseless He became, paralysed with shame.
People marketed the truth naked as glamour
With sentimental anatomy, and life's grammar
In the name of God everything is happening
For the survival of man's life making.

Kathanjali wondered at the philosophical note of the woman, for she traces a life of nothingness save a camouflaged decency.

Kathanjali, who didn't eat anything since many days, felt the pain. Her heart couldn't allow her to eat anything around, but she had to respond to the starving stomach. Burning emptiness of her breadbasket made her faint on the floor, for she couldn't stand anymore. Hunger is natural to anyone, the basic instinct to let the mortal form survive and make the physical form of flesh and blood move forward. No one can abstain from food. May go on fast for many days, but some day, sometime hunger pricks them and they have to yield to it.

Kathanjali, a mother, and a hungry woman now, had to fill her stomach, accumulate some energy and thereby transform it to feed her darling babe. She could not die of hunger for she could not kill her daughter. In vain, she looked for the companions to seek some help. She had to fetch something by hook or crook. She glanced at an old man who was carrying heavy luggage, waiting for a bus on the way. 'Oh! Maybe he is travelling a long distance,' she rationalised. She thought he would have some stuff to fill the stomach. Leaving Prathiksha in a cloth cradle, she advanced towards the man in faltering steps, heart beating faster, flood of questions thronged her mind, but love of mother in her triumphed and she reached him. The traveller turned his face away as if he had seen a bad woman. The behaviour of the traveller melted the frosted grief that gushed through her eyes and rolled on her cheeks. She turned back frustrated and walked towards the hope of her life, who lay cheerfully in the cradle. Every tear on the blackened face in the scorching forenoon reflected many stories.

Poor or tycoon
Same in the mother womb
Pond of blood
A splash so common
Grows fearless
Seems all a game.
Poor or tycoon
Experience the same.
Poor or tycoon
Different in the motherland
Sea of life
A tide so common
One grows coward
Another courageous
War and the game
In the battlefield.
Poor or tycoon
Experience never the same.

While she stepped into the old bad building where she and her daughter were sheltered, burning empty stomach itched with pain, her head ached and she became numb, sat down on the floor, increase in pain made her lone heart yearn for help. In vain, she cried for help. Not knowing what was happening, she cried aloud, but dumb ears of the mortal crowd lost the sense of reception. Unmindful of fellow being in distress, the busy human on the invented machine went on his way exhausting the smoke of indifference. The pain became more than she could endure. She lay down by the road, fighting her best to survive, unconsciously yelled for God, perhaps the decisive comfort she could hope for.

'Oh, God! I cannot fight this life. Save me. Not for my sake but for my daughter, the only companion I have in this world,' she yelled. Her head ached much more, her body rolled around, her head arched backwards gasping for air – the only food she had – her bosom heaved with the wrinkled movements of her body and she finally became unconscious. The heavy truck, which dashed through the way showered her body with mud.

Half dead, Kathanjali felt the droplets of water passing through her dry throat touching the sense organs. She felt the wetness of her eyes, which were swelled in anguish. She raised her brows in slow pace, but they closed as fast as they could, for she was taken aback by the face of a person whose red-hot eyes were showering the scorching heat with fear. 'Oh! He is terrible to look at,' she said to herself. She opened her eyes again as the poured water gave her a life to live again, a life with her daughter. She saw the man holding her mouth in one hand and a mug of water in another. She was shocked to see his hand, exhausted flesh of the fingers to the half, scars so fresh on his arm, a torn cap on his head… 'My goodness! He is a leper,' she denounced him unconsciously with the strength he had given her. He reciprocated with a smile, a smile that unfolded the truth, that he is a fellow human being. The realisation of a neighbour scattered over her mind and pricked her heart to say, 'Thank you... Thanks a lot.' As he heard he roared with laughter and his face slowly turned blue, while beads of tears rolled on Katha's cheeks.

*

They spent time together in exchanging pleasantries of their unpleasant past, cheers for future and denouncing the harsh past in a forgetful mist.

'Wonder what made you come here,' said the man. Katha smiled in response and said, 'What you have guessed is right to some extent.' Katha, whose hunger was still unfulfilled, wanted to satisfy it to the full. Thus she asked the leper without any hesitation. 'Do you have anything to eat?' for she found in him an affection of no attachment.

In response, the leper poured the stuff from his bowl and found conglomeration of different tasks. 'Perhaps national integration,' exclaimed Katha. She took the food hastily and finished the stuff in a few minutes... Then she realised the truth... Hunger knows no taste. When her breadbasket was full, she felt the life in strangeness and expressed her gratitude to the leper.

'Thanks... Thanks a lot... I want to ask you something... Shall I call you grandpa?' Hearing this, the leper rolled in laughter. A laughter of mirth, a happiness of new found relationship. He took her by his hand to the place she was dwelled in.

'What is your name, dear girl?' asked the leper.

Kathanjali smiled at him in pity and said, 'Is there anything in a name?'

'OK. I don't want to argue about it,' the leper responded with a sigh.

'Oh, don't feel bad... I am Katha... Kathanjali.'

'Eh, such a nice name. People call me leper or beggar. I live in leper's colony. I ask for alms till the sunset.'

'Do you go alone all day long?' interrogated Katha.

'We start in groups and we separate to different streets. Later we meet and go home together... By the way, what brought you here to this dungeon place?'

'Dungeon place! After all this is a part of the world.'

The leper laughed at Katha's sense of wit and wondered at her determination even at the trials at peak and said,

'Yes. What you have said is right. Everything is a part of the world, but not us. The way we have been born is same but we still live differently.'

'Grandpa, don't you feel frustrated when people call you a leper.'

'Why should I? I am... I am a leper,' he exclaimed.

'Oh! It's not that. By calling you a leper, they are not accepting you... I mean... as a person.'

'People... People won't accept anyone who is not their kith and kin. So, I was accepted by my kin, who are lepers. After all, we maintain it.'

'Enough of your philosophy, grandpa. You didn't get what I mean exactly. I mean you are called a beggar and you are a leper... People look at you as an outcast from the society... So because of their behaviour and attitude, are you not pinched?'

'Aha, my dear girl. That's what I'm saying. I will feel bad when my clan won't accept me, not when others do... I am a leper... I belong to the leper's colony... My neighbours are lepers... And by profession, I am a beggar.'

The words of the leper touched Katha's heart and made her realise that what grandpa said is true. She had a mother, sister, and a husband to say... but where are they now... she is on a pilgrimage... or say a tramp... her companions are the tramps... whose destination of the journey is not known.

Her daughter, the delight of her heart, darling Prathiksha, is with her because of her age. When she grows up she will mingle with the people whose goal is the same as hers. 'Oh no. No... no... that shall never be. She is the hope of my life... I am living for her... I can't face it... Oh no.... No... She will never part.' The very thought of her honey's parting wounded the heart of Katha and she mused on it for a while.

'Katha... I mean... it seems you are educated. Your mannerism shows that... that is why I...' As she was pondering, Prathiksha woke up and was ready for food.

'Oh, Katha! Let me see your dear daughter,' said the leper.

'Why not grandpa,' so saying Katha kept her daughter in his lap. The leper was taken aback with her behaviour. Unconsciously tears rolled down his cheeks. It was the first time he had touched a non-leper in his life of leprosy. 'Oh, honey! This is enough for my life... let my life end in bliss...' As they were talking, dusk fell and he went to sleep. Cajoling Prathiksha, Katha also slept.

The rays of the sun fell on the eyes of the sleeping Katha as if to wish her good morning. She woke up in joy, a mirth as beautiful as the strength she gained unconsciously from her Grandpa, a true companion and a true source of energy she could look up to. While she mused with gratitude to him, her eyes fell on the cool mortal form of Grandpa, who was not at all bothered of the human bondage in this world. His smiling, sleeping face conveyed the message that he was very much in ecstasy while he slept.

Kathanjali had observed her soiled dress and body, and wished to make herself fresh. She took Prathiksha, who was playing in the cradle, kissed her and said, 'Dear, today I am so happy. Happy because of you... no... no... for you are with me. And in the presence of Grandpa, we can live a life of comfort, a comfortable life indeed... Come, dear one... darling of my heart. Let's take bath before the place gets crowded.' Saying this Katha took best of the two dresses she had, from the sack bag she was carrying and went into the alley by the gutter, where pushing pump made its way through. The pump had many holes and thus fountains the water to the gutter. 'Oh! Sarkar's* service to the down trodden,' she said to herself.

She held Prathiksha in one hand amidst the fall and cleaned her little body with another. Prathiksha danced with cheers, laughing all along. While the rays of the Sun peeped through the alley, cute Prathiksha shimmered as a pearl. Katha wondered at the beauty of her daughter. 'She is beautiful. Oh no... no... beauty self she is.' Later she cleansed herself in the shower, changed her dress and discarded the old one into the gutter as if she was going to start a new life. Perhaps a pure life, and a committed one.

They reached their dwelling and found the leper still sleeping. Sleep, was undisturbed by the hullabaloo of the routine life on the road. Katha wondered the reason for his slumber for he had said that as the sun would rise, he would be on the way for his alms. Anyway, she did not want to disturb Grandpa. She fed Prathiksha and played a while with her, passing a pleasant time all day.

Mother and child
A bond so strong
Strength in spirit
Mirth of the soul
Fullness of the heart
Energy for the while
For mother and child
Even though starving poor.

---

* Government.

The day was scorching with the heat of the sun and humdrum of human life was on the move. The mother and child were tired of playing but their dear Grandpa still didn't rise to shine with the day. Katha unwillingly extended her hands towards Grandpa to wake him up. The physical structure of the leper didn't respond and the hands of Katha felt as chilled as an iceberg.

'Grandpa… Oh, Grandpa. Its afternoon already. Won't you get up today? …Seems he didn't sleep till late night… Anyway, it's too late to be in bed. I'll wake him up.' So saying, Katha woke him up.

Her pulse beat faster and her hand shivered. Dismissing the suspicion from the heart, in vain she cried, 'Oh, Grandpa! What's happened? Are you playing with me? Enough… wake up… it's already noon.'

Unable to restrain her grief and accept the truth, she beat him on his bosom with her fists, slapped him and did all she could. She sought help of the passers-by and in response they denounced her as a trick played by a common beggar. At last, she accepted the truth that he is no more. The nostalgia of her life, with him remained the sweetest part, an incident that taught her parting, a relation which manifested its strength, a lesson which probed into her heart. It was a fellowship that experienced real communion.

While Katha mourned his death, Prathiksha smiled as if one is relieved of the suspense at the end of the play. Grieving Katha couldn't but take refuge in the cheers of her daughter and said,

'Honey
He was with us
He is within us
Life is a stage
Watch every stage
Of each other

Everyone reaches last stage
Honey!
We never met him
Yesteryears
He was with us
Day before
Gave us
Energy in store
He will be
Within us
All the years in store
Of our future world.'

Kathanjali took all the strength from her heart and pondered about the life to be lived and in all respect, she wanted to bid a warm farewell to her Grandpa's mortal form of flesh and bones. So placid, placed on the mud floor. She let the sun set down in the west and the world around take to rest. She took the bowl of her Grandpa to fetch water for his last bath. She mused awhile of the use of bath after one is dead. Her inquisitive mind responded to her heart that one takes bath to clean the physical body one has got. She fetched bowls of water to wash him, took from her sack bag, the only saree which was left and wrapped him in it. She kissed his forehead as a token of farewell, held Prathiksha in one hand and Grandpa's hand in another, drew him across the road while her body sweat in the cool night. She sat down for sometime when she was tired, took all the energy in conviction to finish the job, made her way into an open place through an alley, while dogs barked as she reached the mark. Tired Kathanjali fell for sometime on the ground and gasped for air. Later, she rose and looked for a place to bury the dead body. As she couldn't find any tool to dig the ground, she collected sand and stones from the debris nearby, and piled them on the body. 'It seems to be just another debris,' she said to herself. By the time the cock crowed she was exhausted all her strength to let the mission be complete. Prathiksha looked at her mother with her wide, wild eyes. The very looks of this pretty girl comforted Katha, and in comfort she fell asleep, while Prathiksha set herself to play in full-moon light. Though the space was much, the hard ground didn't allow her a comfortable crawl.

Katha woke up at a distant sound of workers breaking stones, in vain. She searched with her hand for Prathiksha by her side. She got up and looked around and was taken aback by the absence of Prathiksha. She felt an unbearable pain. Not knowing what to do, she yelled for her daughter and ran in hurried steps in search of her. She looked around and walked till the workplace, inquired the workers who were spending time with an astrologer. No one responded positively, rather they were harsh at her for she had disturbed them as well as the parrots of the astrologer. She turned back in hope, sat down in the mid-way but eyes moving around for a sight of her dear daughter. Suddenly she heard a voice calling her. 'O ye woman, wait... wait there.' A man in colourful robes from head to heels came near her. She recognised him to be the astrologer who was with the workers. Moments later, he was by her side. He sat down beside her and inquired about her problem. He looked into her eyes in utmost seriousness, as if he was going to prophesise her daughter's whereabouts. He asked the name of the girl, uttered some magical verses and offered his help in her search for Prathiksha. Each went in different directions. As the astrologer moved a bit forward, he saw a little girl sobbing amidst the sandstones, perhaps tired of crying all the hours. He rushed to the girl, Prathiksha, and when he was about to take the girl, a thought sprang in his mind. A thought so commercial but very true to his profession. He returned to Katha who was still searching in hope and asked her to co-operate with him to find the baby by invoking spirits.

He took the magical wand, waved it around and threw it in the direction where he saw Prathiksha was. He closed his eyes and said, 'Look, dear woman, the spirit is so gracious unto you. It answered the prayers in swiftness to show the way to your daughter. The spirit is aware that your daughter is so precious to you, and so it kept your daughter alive amidst the sandstones.' A moment later he opened his eyes and asked Katha to follow him. Katha followed him without any hesitation to the place he took her. As they both went nearer, Katha's eyes fell on Prathiksha, who was very tired by now. She rushed towards her, kissed her all over her face and thus poured out her affection upon her darling daughter. Then she fed the baby in haste. The astute astrologer who tried his best to pretend as a holy man said, 'The spirit, I believe, heard our prayers for she is so gracious to you.'

Kathanjali fell on his feet in humble adoration and thanked him with due respect. He raised her, wiped her tears and said,

'Where are you heading to?'

'I don't know,' answered Katha.

'Seems your journey knows no destination.'

'Yes, Swamiji, I am a deserted one. My only hope is my daughter. I want to live my life for her.'

The astrologer who wanted to make use of the most, closed his eyes in sombre devotion and said, 'Daughter, the spirits are merciful to you. I'll show you your destination. You should be here to be thankful unto her.'

'O, Swamiji, I am. I'll be... forever,' saying Katha touched his feet in devotion.

## Chapter Four

# Faith and Betrayal

Kathanjali, Prathiksha and the astrologer travelled long on foot, through busy streets of the town, halting hither and thither to tell a tale as a part of his business, or relaxed sometimes with a sip of tea by the roadside. At last, they reached the railway station. They went in onto the platform and got into the train. The train looked like a deserted one and was about to move in an hour, as told by the authorities. The astrologer seemed to be a person who has travelled and was aware of the rules of the track. Kathanjali fed Prathiksha and made her lie on the wooden bench, but was restrained by the astrologer. She was asked to go to the end of the coach and take the last bench, a safe place to get down. Meanwhile, the place was crowded with passengers of varied kind, a strange experience for Katha, as that was the first time she got into a train.

Katha tried a lot to inquire the astrologer of many things. But he was very busy to answer her a single word as he had a tough time to satisfy the customers amidst the train passengers, who stretched their palms at him to know something interesting and were inclined to his word of prophesy. Tired Kathanjali slept on the floor in deep slumber. Starved Prathiksha disturbed Katha's sleep and woke her up. In uneasiness, she looked for Swamiji in disguise, and was relieved on seeing him around. The astrologer came near Katha and sat by her. Katha wished to be relieved of the suspense about the destination of her journey. Her blind faith restrained her from asking such a silly question, but her intuitive mind strained itself through faith-stricken heart. Thus, she said, 'Swamiji, where have we to get down?' The astrologer reciprocated with a smile as if she passed a question of silliness. 'I stay at Reyepuram. I stay alone now. There…' answered the astrologer.

'I couldn't get what you said…'

'The spirit is so gracious unto you that I received a divine command to look after you. You look after myself… I'll look after you.'

'Praise be the spirit… Shall I know in what name I'll pray to the spirit?' inquired Katha.

'O ye women, you are anxious to know… I have been worshipping this spirit right from the moment my mother conceived me. I'll be worshipping forever…till my body turns to ash… my soul mingles with the spirit and then I'll consume you,' blah blahed the astrologer.

Katha wondered at the vague concept of his talk of her simple question – where are we heading? Moreover, her faith in his answers grew much more. She believed in his divinity. All the time she was musing over the dilemma of her state, when the astrologer played with Prathiksha.

The ticket inspector approached them. He was wished with cheerfulness of familiarity by the astrologer. Katha wondering at the behaviour of man in black suit, gayness that enveloped both the men, she confirmed her faith in the greatness of the astrologer, as many a passenger thronged the T.I. with their humble requests, but he was in the company of the Swami. They chatted for sometime. When enquired about Katha and Prathiksha, he took the T.I. to a side and whispered something. Later, the T.I. made his way on his business, while the astrologer reworded his philosophy to stabilise his position in her heart as a divine aesthetic.

'Swamiji, is that man the boss of this vehicle?' asked Katha with ignorance.

'Of course he is. He visits me for every problem in his life. Now he was here to check put the ticket-less travellers.'

'Oh, my God. We don't have tickets. What to do?' worried Kathanjali.

'Don't worry, o ye woman. If he is the boss of the train, I am the one who guides him in his journey of life. You know I am the one who predicted his job when he was a toddler. As long as I am with you, no one questions you,' uttered the satanic man.

Poor Kathanjali faithfully listened to him and his morphine behaviour. She forgot to feed her daughter. She was blindfolded by the serpentine guile of the astrologer. For a thought of common sense, she depended on him, and he magnified a tiny issue to make herself nothing. In him she took refuge.

Travel
Through
Hills and valleys
Blindfolded faith
Unknown destination
'Follow me'
That rocked life 'strife'
For
A maid of no-self
Travelling
Ticketless.

*

At last they reached their destination. A destiny, which rocked her life and she never dreamt that she was to be crushed. Crushed for fragrance, a perfume of real self, to rock the world with her camouflaged appearance.

They got down from the train and walked straight by the railway track for a few minutes. Kathanjali holding Prathiksha, unconsciously turned right which lead to the main road. Astrologer called back, hinted her their way is left and asked her to simply follow him. He made his way through a crowded street on the left side, walked long, crossed a drain and finally stopped at an old hose, fenced with wood. He then led the mother and daughter in, offered them a glass of water and snacks to eat.

'O ye woman, your works starts tonight and is an easy job to do,' said the astrologer. Katha, with gratitude, looked at him in wonder. How merciful he is? 'Swamiji, may I know the kind of work I have to do, 'cos I had an easy hand only in work of household and in nothing else.'

'Do not worry, dear woman. It is a work of common sense and you need not strain your hands as you used to do.'

'...But Swamiji... work without straining hands... It's a wonder. I am a bit confused.'

'To be candid, you have to sell your flesh,' straight answered Swamiji.

'Swamiji, you mean it...' exclaimed Katha.

Astrologer could not hold his laugh at the funniest answer of Kathanjali. He asked the ignorant Katha to wait till the sun sets down and then she herself will come to know of work she has to do. In the afternoon, he offered her a sumptuous lunch that she never had before and asked her to take rest, so that she could work without a diversion of sleep. Kathanjali couldn't get even a little of the work he said she had to do. With a blind belief upon the astrologer and his spirit, she thought of waiting for the job and was happiest creature. She was going to live on her own. She praised the spirit and glorified the astrologer as the God-sent angel.

'O woman, I am going out. By twilight you set yourself for the job. Don't worry, any sort of job on the first day makes anyone nervous. Spirit will be upon you. You take bath and beautify your looks. Not that you are not beautiful, you know, but beauty never matters. Only the power of attraction that draws many. OK dear woman, I'll be back with an assignment. Get ready, OK.' Kathanjali bewildered at the long teaching he gave her. She suffered from confrontation of thoughts that rose within her.

She couldn't find any reason why all this is needed to sell meat. Moreover, it was a wonder that a sale of meat… during night… with beautification… attraction. 'Oh, my God. Whatever will be, will be.' Suddenly her eyes fell on Prathiksha, who was now six months old, and infant who lived slice of her life in sun and shower, tasted everything bitter, yet she has grown more sweeter.

Katha dismissed all thoughts of her job for she had to live on her own, not for herself but for her darling daughter, the delight of her eyes. She vowed on her daughter that she would never let the future of Prathiksha be in confrontation. She decided to do anything, any venture, better or worse for the smooth sail of Prathiksha's life.

Kathanjali took bath as he said, wore the garment he gave, painted her face, glittered her cheeks, fixed flowers in her hair, polished her nails, looked into the mirror and couldn't hold her laughter. 'All these things to sell meat. OK. In his words, to sell flesh. Aha.'

She took Prathiksha in her hands, looked into her wide, wild eyes. When she looked straight into them, she couldn't restrain her tears, 'cos she had to leave her alone for sometime, at least during her work. The very thought made her to burst out in tears. 'No… no… no… I will never leave my daughter alone and go on my work. What if she is with me? The job I have is to sell flesh and if this girl stays with me, she will give me company when no one is there to buy flesh… Anyhow she too will learn the business. When she grows she will be a master in the trade… Shut up… What a stupid thought… My girl is innocent. She is the honey and the sweetest of my heart. She will be good and reach the greatest heights in her life... Yes... yea if she is with me, unconscious mastering of the trade may envelop her. I'll let her stay away for her sake. I'll sacrifice my pleasure of her company for her good... Oh, my face...beautified...got spoiled. It is time for his return.'

Leaving Prathiksha, Katha who is ignorant of the job, had to set her make up right and wait for Swamiji's return, who promised that he would be back with his consignment. She walked to the door anticipating his return and was taken aback by a wayward youth commenting.

'O, a new one!'

'Seems to me as a holy bitch,' chorused another.

She was taken aback by the remarks of the passers-by and the 'New one' puzzled her much. The more she thought, much more confused was her state.

Katha became tensed than ever and could predict her position in future world as a great challenge. Her frightened heart was comforted by warm looks of her daughter. As she pondered, the astrologer entered with a grey-haired, frail person, whose clothes would weigh more than his body. He took him into a room upstairs exchanging pleasantries, while Katha looked on in amazement. A few minutes later, he came down and called Katha.

'O woman, are you ready for the job?' he asked her in all smiles.

'Yes, Swamiji, I am. As you had said. But may I know exactly what kind of job I have to do? Seems people around here are mere filth.'

'Stop nonsense. No one is filthy in your business,' he was annoyed. 'But Swamiji, I cannot understand...'

'Ah... Eh, woman, remember one thing – Customer is the king – should be the rule of the business,' remarked the astrologer. 'I beg your pardon, Swamiji. I am not able to understand your high sounding phrases. It is too difficult for this common woman to comprehend...'

'Yea... Here you are... For a common woman to comprehend, let me tell you. You are a common woman, but it does not matter whether you are common or noble. It is enough, provided you should have a trickery of a smile. OK. That's all you need for a successful trader,' said the astrologer.

Katha was much more puzzled with the kind of words he uttered, like 'a trickery of a smile'. She came to senses with a command of Swamiji to take food and get ready for the job. Tensed Katha was reminded that Prathiksha would be a disturbance, so she lullabied her to sleep.

Kathanjali served herself supper, but she could not taste a bit for she was taken over by confusion of her state. 'How I wish that I would have stayed back by the highway at the old bad building,' she sighed.

'O woman... did you finish the meal?' said the astrologer from upstairs.

'Yes, Swamiji, I have,' answered Katha.

'Leave the girl downstairs... and you come up,' said the astrologer.

Katha obeyed his words faithfully for she believed that he was the one who helped her find Prathiksha, he was the one who showed her the way to live. With trembling feet she climbed the stairs, with a question mark on every step. When she was up, Swamiji looked at her... blessed her with magic wand. 'May you reap bounty of harvest and let my pocket be full with your grateful wiles.' Afterwards he made his way down thumping the door on her face.

Wondered Katha's ears responded to a sound from a room by the door. It was the voice of that frail old man calling her. 'Eh... you do not waste my time... I can't sleep late night... come and sit by me.' Desperate Katha, who now knew the kind of job she had to do was much frustrated and concluded that the gracious spirit was nothing but demonic. As she was kissed up in dear situation, the frail man limped forward and dragged her for an indecent proposal of that common act. The weakling figure of this old creature could not withstand the strength of the will power, and had but to prostrate on the floor. Katha hurried downstairs, in vain she tried to open the closed door. She yelled wildly and was subsided in roaring silence. The astrologer opened the door with Prathiksha in her hand. He smiled at her, wiped her tears dry with his turban, and said, 'Your hope is in my hand, if you turn against me, you'll be hopeless, and in hopelessness, you will be entangled in this place... You do the job I have entrusted... be happy with your daughter, otherwise... hope I need not repeat again... Go my dear woman... lie with him and live in happiness.' Saying so, he slammed the door on her face. The entangled dame was confronted by the attachment to her daughter and the price of self-respect. She climbed back thinking of her daughter.

Boat
Made by paper
By a tender hand
Proud of her masters
Loved the piece

Left it
For a smooth sail
In a pool
Stood still

Darkened sky
Gave out tornado
Disease stricken dame
Shivered
Hurried out
For sailing herself

For

A boat
Made of paper
'Cos
Shapeless
It'll be
Hopeless
She will remain
        Tender hand
        Proud of her mastery
        Loved the piece

She approached. Noticed his welcoming shivering hand stretched forth, responded, lay by him like a bundle of cotton wool and spend the night weeping while he was found cheerfully sleeping.

*

As the light of the moral world rose in east of the sky, Katha went downstairs and noticed the astrologer with a cup of tea in his hand. 'Good morning, dear woman… How's the job?' he inquired. She paced inside without answering him. He followed her and offered her tea. She was astonished at the treatment she was being offered, took Prathiksha to her bosom and hugged her tight, pouring out her affection conveying how she missed her last night. The astrologer came near her, pat her on back and said; 'You are a woman of convictions, do not make any haste and walkout… This is my place. I can pick you up anywhere… OK… Now go and offer this porridge to the man upstairs.'

She went to the man to offer him morning breakfast. He lay on the bed in deep slumber, snoring to the top. She sat down on the floor, thinking of the exit from that mire. She was convinced that he no longer believed her and even kept his eye on every moment of hers.

'Why not I... when he is out... he will not go anywhere... if he doesn't go, then who will arrange for the consignment toady... yes, that's the right time of which I have to make best use of... if he locked me up inside. What shall I do now?' Suddenly she remembered his philosophical lecture on trickery of smile and in the very next moment, she was on cloud nine and praised herself for her inquisitiveness.

'Eh... woman what are you doing there... this girl is crying,'' yelled the astrologer. 'I'll be down in a moment... perhaps she is hungry,' saying this she went down, fed the baby in haste and lullabied her to sleep. The silence that enveloped the whole room was disturbed by the entrance of the old man, previous night's client, who came downstairs. Noticing him, the astrologer wished him in all honour and requested his forgiveness for all the inconveniences caused. As the old man was about to open his mouth to pass a remark, Katha, summing up all her strength, drew near him and kissed him on his cheek, acknowledging his return, and turned back at the astrologer playing trickery of smile. Surprised astrologer's joy knew no bounds. He hugged Kathanjali and called her a golden apple. Later they bade farewell to the client and settled themselves with relief.

By twilight, she beautified her body as he had instructed her. She called the astrologer who was still having his nap.

'Swamiji, won't you go out to fix up the consignment for today... I am getting ready for the job... so...' The astrologer woke up to foot and said, 'I am sorry that I have misunderstood you... you... are... a golden apple.' He went out in all happiness to fetch a much costlier client, promising her a feast that night for her maiden success.

Kathanjali took a few dresses, which he had brought as outfits for her trade and a few currency notes offered as a tip by the old man last night, took sleeping Prathiksha in her arms and stepped out through the backdoor. She then made her way through an alley that people use to shit.

She inquired at the railway station about the train on the platform, paid for the ticket to the terminal halt of the train, got in and hid in the toilet till the train started to move.

Unknown journey
Ends somewhere
Unknown
In knowledge of time
Turns to be known.

*

The train reached the destination, travelling for a continuous hours breaking hither and thither meanwhile. It was a sunny morning, so fresh and gay in all lives of village green. Most of the flock appeared to be very common. The railway station was situated by the fields of the village, an irrigation canal passing through. Farmers were seen working with their sickles and ploughs. While few oldies were enjoying smoke leaning onto the palm tree. The scene was so strange and refreshing when compared to the congested lanes and stinking pissing alleys of Reyepuram.

# Chapter Five

# Guilt

Kathanjali, who was relieved of the mire, was released but haunted by the dilemma about the mission she had to accomplish. She had to fetch a job somehow to win her bread and live on her own. She looked out for a parlour to have coffee to refresh her body tired out of long journey. She got into a waiting room for a bath, refreshed herself and walked out to discover the town.

She was moving in a slow pace with Prathiksha in her arms and a bundle of dresses in her hand. 'Everybody is a busy body here,' she said to herself. She walked by a canal where wooden boats were anchored, fish big and small were dried up on the river bank, people dwelling in mud huts, none dressed below the knees, most of them found to be workers with the mud. On the other side of the river, the road – perhaps a highway – was thronged with bullock carts and bulky motor vehicles. She walked a few yards before the path turned right, through huge trees on either side, whose branches darkened the way, not letting a ray of sun peep into. It was altogether a different scene. A flock of people was working with bamboos, speaking a different dialect from the others. She continued to walk on the way left and finally onto a small bridge to cross the canal. She stepped on the main road, busy indeed with shops and people gathered around, and bought a bag at a cheaper rate to keep her clothes. There was a bus stop nearby, where people carrying their baggage were getting down from hired man pulling rickshaws.

Suddenly she glanced at a shop selling lace, a place so popular for the product. She went, posed herself as a wealthy lady leading a simple life and bargained for a piece of lace. While bargaining she enquired the salesman of the manufacturing centres of lace. She chatted with him for a few minutes on issues of regional importance, meanwhile extracting all information of local flavour. When the clock struck twelve, she strolled to a restaurant nearby, had lunch and later left in a rickshaw for a charity home. She met the supervisor and expressed her quest for some work, giving out all her abilities.

'Where do you come from?' he enquired

'From eastern end of the state' she answered

'What has brought you here all the way?'

'I have lost my family in a rail accident…I live on my purse. …A gentleman directed me to this place and assured me that I would be benefited from this institute.' Katha tried to convince the man.

'Aha... no one comes here with a different story… one gentleman directed… benefited… promising to be a faithful… absconding finely… all this I have been listening since I joined here.' He was annoyed. And Katha was taken aback by such a reaction of the person.

She pleaded with him to believe her and tried to convince that she was ready to do any sort of job she was offered. To her surprise, he called for the gatekeeper and ordered him to throw her out. In response, the gatekeeper obeyed him without a word but was restrained by a cool confronting voice. The entire place became alert and everyone was attentive. A frail woman in her sixties, who had been living in that place for quite a long time, entered wearing a garment of cheap texture. She was also the founder of that charity home. She probed Katha, as an interrogative policeman would, save in cool temper, not hurting the sentiments or feelings, and at last, found something truthful in her.

'OK, Kathanjali. I believe you. Hereafter you work as my personal maid. You and your child can stay in my quarters… I repeat… I believe you.' The very words touched Katha's heart as a source of energy that the best of any medication couldn't match. She was led into Madam's quarters and was instructed by an old man there, about the work she was to do.

'Look young girl… you have to keep Madam's room clean, wash the soiled clothes, always be at her reach to hand her whatever… whenever she wants. OK. I repeat.' And he repeated the same. Then he drew closer and whispered, 'You seem to be very innocent. Work hard and win Madam's confidence… she loves hard workers… if any doubt you ask me… OK, dear girl.'

*

'Kathanjali felt the newness of life in every movement and every moment. The work she had to attend on was quite homely and in vicinity. She dwelled in so calm with spiritual fervour.

She had a lot of time to spend with her daughter, in all pleasures of motherliness. Faltering step, chirpy words and childish pranks of Prathiksha amused everyone and Madam had a special favour for this growing girl in her heart. Time, fleeting thief of childhood, ended soon, passing haste in norms of modern world. Madam found a necessity to impose a hardship on the cute young lass with a slate and a pencil. Scribbling hand and inquisitive mind attracted Madam, who planned along with her mother, to admit the little girl in a boarding school in the same town. Parting is painful indeed, but a meeting at every weekend gave a hope of life to the mother and daughter.

Katha spent her days with Madam in faith and with her obedience and commitment won her favour, while jealousy and indifference of her fellow-workers. One night before going to bed Madam called Kathanjali to her room to chat with her. She said that she had a bad headache and asked her to soothe it by applying a lotion with her healing hands. They exchanged pleasantries and indulged in intense discussion on religion. They concluded that people kill each other for the sake of revenge and not religion.

Katha was the best of servants and Madam the best of employers. The chit-chat of pleasantries turned serious with Madam's question, 'Where did you work before?'

Katha was a bit hesitant to answer, had confrontation over the right answer that arose no suspicions in the love and motherly affection. Katha no more wanted to hide her past. So she confessed before Madam her life which was never smooth.

'Is the story which you have said true?'

'Yes! Why should I fabricate?'

'Where did you bury all this stinking stuff?'

'I didn't, but scented with perfume of forgetfulness.'

'Do you still hope for your husband's return?'

'I do... 'cos the only man I have loved is the father of my daughter and it is he.'

'Did Prathiksha never ask for her father?'

'Rarely... she has never felt the touch of his love, but she feels unfulfilled when ever she looks at her friend's parents...she feels wounded when watching her friends' fathers visiting them in school.'

'I pity you, dear Katha... What do you answer her?'

'Oh, Madam! It's quite normal. Visiting time is short and I simply divert the topic.'

'Do you think so?'

'I know I do. But I can't help the situation... and the diversion is not to divert my daughter's quest for her father but for my sake... I never get out of bed without wishing him good morning... even though I know very much he is not with me.'

'Oh, Katha. Didn't you ever hate him?'

'Aha. I hated him. And later, I hated him with a violent passion. I never expected the same feelings from him, as I knew the truth.'

'Truth…?'

'Yes, Madam, I was the passion fruit for him and he ate it and I experienced his roots, so I want to cherish him.'

'Did you ever write to him how you love him?'

'Oh, Madam, I was young. I feel love is to be manifested and not to be spoken of. If he really panted for me, wouldn't he be back by now? The one who praised my tone forgot me when I finished the song. I never felt my tone is to entertain anyone.'

'I am sorry Kathanjali. I had never expected a grave past from you… I know you are living for Prathiksha and she is the hope of your life… I will sponsor her education till the very end and she will show you a way… But I myself feel like strangling the bastard to death.'

'Oh, Madam… I am sorry, but never call him by such filthy name. I still love him.'

'Oh, Katha… But I envy that man.'

'OK, Madam, it is already 1 a.m.… Late sleep is not good for your health.'

'Good night, Katha.'

'Good night, Madam.'

Time rolled on in happiness and spread on the lives in routine, nothing special, as usual marked the minds of the people. Lace curtains, cotton mattress, visiting hours, conversing with visitors, chatting with inmates, answering phone calls, a talk tool for Katha for her experiences, fruit juice and wasted meat, seldom a peg of wine looking at gold watch in leisure made the life of Madam. Quite joyful as her very name conveys Madam Joy… Early rise from bed, arranging a flower rose, receiving visitors, visiting Prathiksha at weekend, looking for an order handy to Madam Joy. All the acts haunted by a hope for her hubby was Kathanjali's daily routine.

Everything went on without a hindrance till Madam Joy's gold watch was lost. It was so precious to Madam that she kept is as a souvenir of love from her father. Though the watch stopped working long time ago, love for the watch was conveyed and was still alive in her heart.

One winter afternoon, which marked the turn of six years in Katha's life with the Madam, Madam Joy stretched her hand to the stool as she revived from a doze. She was bewildered, as she couldn't find the watch. She was very depressed at the state of loss. She called Kathanjali and informed her. Katha was taken aback and much shocked at Madam's condition. She sent for people to search all over the premises, where Madam had gone for a stroll and chatted with inmates. They searched everywhere, under the blanket, in the wardrobe and even the soap-case in the toilet. Madam kept shedding tears all the time and ate nothing.

One of the oldest family friends of Madam Joy suggested checking the belongings of all inmates and workers. But they couldn't find the watch anywhere. When everything was searched save Katha's room, all eyes fell on her. One of them went ahead to search her belongings but was restricted by Madam.

'What do you think you are doing?' Madam restricted.

'We have searched everywhere, including our own belongings. Only Katha's room is left.'

'I haven't been to Katha's room since many days. How can you think that I could have left it there?'

'You didn't visit ours either, but even our closets were not spared.'

'Shut up, you filthy stuff. What do you think of Kathanjali? She is as truthful as burnt iron. She has always been truthful to me. The very truth is her life. Never even think of suspecting her.' But Madam Joy's friend was still trying to convince her. 'When everybody is under suspicion then why so you spare this woman… after all she is a servant here. Moreover, to err is human, you know.'

'Oh, dear old friend! Believe me. To err may be a human weakness but not Katha's. I have confidence in her. To suspect her is to suspect myself.'

When everyone was angry about the discrimination Madam made, she succumbed to their plea, saying, 'I will permit you to check Katha's belonging not to prove her innocence, but to prove my confidence and faith in her. I never treated her as my servant. She too loved me as a daughter and was as affectionate as a friend.' All the inmates were very cheerful at the advent of Katha's ouster while Madam Joy and Katha were very confident. Their confidence on each other and themselves whiffed in a flash as the gold watch was found in Katha's wooden case.

Shocked at being in such a situation, Katha shivered and looked at the butler with fear. While the inmate's joy was complete, Madam Joy's grief knew no bounds. She still couldn't believe her eyes. She was her confidante. She was so kind to her. Moreover she loved her with a love which was more than love. She couldn't open her mouth to speak, but her silver tears reflected much of her sorrow. She didn't raise her hand for her to be thrown her out, but she couldn't look at her either. She didn't do anything, for she couldn't.

Silence reigned the quarters. Madam Joy's roaring heart, filled with love turned violent, was suppressed by love itself. Perhaps love files no record of wrongdoing. Taking all the strength, she held Katha's chin in her hand and said with a choked voice,

'Did you do it, Katha? I know you are not the one… is it not…? Katha, my dearest one, answer me…' Katha, wounded with guilt, ran away and never saw Madam Joy again.

She stepped into the railway station, longing to see Prathiksha, but restrained herself, 'cos there was nothing to worry. There was money deposited for good in her name. Let her live in goodness and no sparks of guilt ignite her heart. Yes, she should be good all through her life, she shouldn't be disturbed because of her mother's guilt.

She didn't have a paisa to buy a ticket, where to go remained the question. If she stays for some more time, she thought, 'People would chase me… that culprit butler cheated me. Leave it. I can't stay here anymore. The violent winds of guilt knock me down… Oh! There comes the train… Let me go in… But I don't have any money to buy a ticket with… come on… what will be, will be…'

## Chapter Six

# Flesh Trade Unlimited

Having travelled for long, at last the train halted at the terminal station. She had to get down. 'Why not I go back... if I get down here, where to go... let me go out and see... Oh, my God! It is Reyepuram... You senseless stupid, it is Reyepuram.'

When she peeped through the glass panes of the toilet, she saw green fields, working farmers and children playing, who reflected the innocence that she had lost a day ago. Masticating cattle seemed to be spitting on her faithfulness. Her surrender to the butler's blackmail for sake of her self-respect made her lose respect in herself completely. Her relation with Madam, that was stronger than the umbilical cord itself, strangled her love. Her running away would imply she cheated Madam Joy by giving more weight to temptation than to love. Though the love she found in Madam was very firm and she was not able to forget it.

Longing to see
Vacuum of rib
She
Longing
Of heart's beat
To be heart
For one
Is unknown
Distance

Longing
To end
Life's strife
Of lone heart's
Whisper
Longing
To answer
Her offspring
Of her cause
That left
Unanswered.

It was midnight and no one was in sight. She sat at the end of the long platform looking into the darkness. She could easily trace her dark sin in light of dark night. She spent three days and nights, but to become a plaything of porters and people of all sorts.

Though she was fed with comments so filthy, teasing so terrible, her breadbasket was dried up and looked for something to satisfy itself. She begged and tried all the ways, hoped for life, and was prepared to endure at all costs. Suddenly the philosophy of the astrologer and prostration of the old man flashed in her mind. 'Let's play the trickery of smile,' she said to herself.

She adjusted her folded saree, washed her face, sat cross-legged on a bench and stared around. She was led into a goods wagon for a fistful of coins.

While she sipped coffee, she dipped an oldie for the show. The taxicab dashed into a large house where she lived for life.

Hunger
Made her
Welcome an unknown
Cigars ash

Dominate
Incense stick
Burned
To give out
Perfume
Prostrate
Strained legs
Stretched wide
To fulfil one's hunger
Thus
To satisfy hers.

With a handful of money she earned in the darkness of night, she strolled to a shop, bought garments and food stuff to make her human engine survive.

She roamed all over the town for a work to live, reached station with a despair of rejection. Her happiness increased when in a conversation she came to know that the astrologer was no more.

She slept a sound sleep, perhaps tired of sleeplessness or because of the contented joy of learning the news of his death. She was not perturbed by anyone till break of the day. She walked through labyrinth of crowded commercial places, requesting, pleading and begging for a work to live, halted at a restaurant for lunch, satisfied her hunger, counted the leftover currency notes, strolled back to station. She walked through a lane with houses roofed with asbestos sheets, to cut the way short. While she was passing, a voice called from a house by the way. She looked back and found no one, so she walked along. Again the voice called her. She responded to the same, entered in, found a woman so tall, well-built, wore a shirt half-hooked, cloth strips of her skirt to fasten her waist fairly low.

She asked Katha to take a chair with an ecstatic smile, holding a magazine in her hand that pressed against her breast.

'I've been seeing you loitering on the platform. What's up with you?' inquired the woman.

'What's it to you if I roam or broom on a platform? It is a public place,' replied an annoyed Katha.

'Aha. Public place… so clever… I need people like you… you shrewd whore.'

'Mind your language… I am Katha… Kathanjali.'

'Shut your mouth, you alley cat. I have been staying here since twenty years… Still I am the rose of many heart-stricken bastards. You stay with me and I will make you a rose of the city,' convinced Musali.

'I am living not for my sake but for hope. I hope to see…'

'Oh enough… enough. Sentiments and feelings don't have a place here. They are the obstacles for the business.'

'I'll let you know afterwards,' saying so, Katha left the place.

'You'll come to me,' assured Musali. Katha went back to the platform, sat on the bench and mused for a while.

'Where have you been last night… you tired of… why don't you speak…' said somone.

'Oh… let her be yaar, seems she got screwed up so tight,' replied another.

'Are you looking for… come on… do not worry. I won't bargain.'

All these things wounded her much and she rushed to Musali in a quick pace. Musali hugged her and kissed her ruby red lips.

'You will no longer live on the parched pavement, occupy one of the huts here… do not demean them. Huts are mobile, isn't it? Even though they are huts, they have the comfort of every type.'

'Eh, Ranga… keep that new hut clean and tidy. Katha… this is Katha, new flower of our garden… she'll occupy that.'

'Seems you are very prosperous… got everyone at your beck and call,' Katha exclaimed.

'Ah prosperous. We can lead life… how one makes it. You know people call me whore… a bazaar woman… if I step into that stinking Royal Hospital… young docs who can't hold stethoscope with their fingers call me an untouchable.'

'Oh! My Goodness!'

'Do not mind, Katha… I never mind. It comes with the trade… and trade is our life. OK, let this thing be brought up later. Let me tell you the secret of our trade.'

'Trickery of smile,' Katha giggled.

'Oh! You are a master. I need not teach you.' With joy Musali hugged Katha, and gave her a treat of wine and fried peanuts.

'You know, Katha, I am a vegetarian.'

'And you trade flesh, aha,' countered Kathanjali.

Katha was led into the hut she was allowed. It was a small place. A 2 feet by 4 feet room, a ceiling fan, a cot and a pitcher of water made a living place quite mobile. She lay on the bed and thought of her new life. Tears rolled as she remembered Madam Joy and a spontaneous flow of curse on the ruthless butler. He robbed that timepiece and asked Kathanjali to keep it. When she replied he blackmailed her that he overheard her conversation with Madam and was very much aware of her past, and he would make it public. Moreover he would let the story be known in the school and hostel where Prathiksha was boarding. For the sake of name and fame, she agreed with him and was the part of deception. How sharp is the guilt that haunted her every time… one should be away from it.

'Katha… eh Katha… you bloody… Open the door.'

Katha opened the door and was angry at the way she was called for. 'What do you think of me?'

'I think the same what I think of myself. We are in the same family. You will get used to it. Here no one calls you with those cute, sweet names. We have to feel the stink of life. Stink will be made sweet and much sweeter in course if life… Hey, come on, yaar… It's fine. Get ready. Musali has sent these for you.'

Katha was much amused at the state of things. She liked that girl. Moreover her 'no' attracted her. Nagini… She is a damsel of very young age and is a master in her craft.

'Eh! You like indoors or outdoors… You see the men over here are rotten and rough… need not worry much about them. Let time pass, in mere words, with them you can be least tired of the game.'

While Nagini spoke, Katha got herself ready and she looked gorgeous in her dazzling garment.

'Oh! You are ready for the show. Come on.' Nagini took her to a place every eye fell on Katha and she felt something mysterious about it. Her modern ways and sharp eyes made the way flocked with her beauty. Her slender waist left many spellbound.

Suddenly, a woman in a dress, which was less than a cloth, hugged her lightly, smacked her cheek and said, 'Let me know about you, dear one.'

'Do not worry, she is a lesbian,' pacified Nagini, to wipe out her confusion.

She was sent with a client who seemed to be pretty rich and old in age.

Painted face
Thick lipstick
Glittered cheek
Shimmered garment
Poisonous perfume

Darkened night
Led the unknown
For a known act
Heartless feelings
Cursed sweet moan
Colder kisses
Bitter hugs
Suffocating chill
Burn the desire
With contagious ash
Lets out a stink
Left as he in blue
Leaving a blue note.

Years passed in her stay at Reyepuram, with people quite normal, frustrated with lives, hardship of Musali, infectious diseases, suppressed self-respect, taskmaster so terrible, hardships to endure.

*

Musali, the queen of Reyepuram, always had a feeling for the workers' welfare. She lay on bed to have a nap after a hectic schedule of meeting with police people, conversation with Inspector Razack, release of few workers on bail, deliberations with confidants to raise the revenue etc. She was disturbed with the entrance of Nagini and was astonished at her furious rage. She offered Nagini a glass of water and inquired the reason for her anger.

'Madam, we wish to take a procession in the city to remind the rest that we are part of them,' replied Nagini. Musali laughed at the idea and said that she did not find any reason to remind the people for they themselves visit the place. She tried to convince Nagini that the idea was foolish and the procession would be a futile attempt.

'Oh Madam, we are here not for our pleasure. We are here to work for food... for survival... for life. We are serving and in return receiving the payment. We are not being paid out of charity.' Nagini's outburst of anger paused as Kathanjali entered the room. They shared many hard feelings of their life and resolved to fight for their right to be called as a very worker, very labourer, whose primary idea was to earn a decent livelihood. They were not called by their name... In fact, they are to be named themselves to suit the ear of a client. They pondered for hours, chalked out the programme and convinced Musali to approve. They both danced with joy when she approved.

The problem started with a policeman who interrogated one of the inmates regarding her parents. Poor girl who never saw them, the very word 'parent' was very foreign to her, and she could not answer. He laughed at her, spat on her, stripped her clothes with a victorious smile, calling her filthy bitch. And the same evening he was at her hut bargaining with a request to satisfy him. She thought of accepting but restrained herself with a logical conclusion that she may lose even those fistful of currency notes for she may not serve more than one, 'cos she was beaten so hard by that man.

*

The meeting was convened in an open ground of Reyepuram and they had banned all the services offered by them. The busy bees of Reyepuram gathered together and were happy for they felt it was a long awaited holiday from their strenuous work. Nagini stood and addressed the gathering,

'My dear sisters, who have never had a brother, I wish you all a pleasant evening. Today is a great day for us. We have to make use of it. We all have assembled here to fight for our rights. We don't know our parents. We are brought here through many means. This is our home... our nation... our world. If we go out to clean our organs, which are soiled by those sanctified people, we are looked upon as stray dogs and alley pigs. We are branded as carriers of diseases... can we cultivate a disease on our own... we cannot... but with the help of those holy peers with a filthy mouth calling us bitches. They are paying us for charity. They are paying us minimum for the maximum service of pleasure we offer them. We are denied right to vote... to elect a government, but they will use us to grab the voters... to get their work done... to defame a person to improve the other's fame and name. When the time comes to file an application for an identity card to get ration, we are denied it for we have left out the column of father's name or husband's name. We are living in this nation but we are not a part of it. So, my dear sisters, we are far better. In fact, we are holier than those women who go to any extent to fulfil their desires. We are branded as contributors of immoral traffic for we are working for our food with a given designation 'prostitute'. Are we any immoral than those women who go astray and be unfaithful to their wedded husbands. Are we any immoral than those men who visit us often and take us to their house in their spouse's absentia. We are more lawful for we are true to our profession. We have every right to fight for our rights and speak moral, though we are branded as immoral than those unfaithful husbands and wives who do such things in darkness. So, we have to fight for our right to vote, against discrimination in the society as stray people. We may not know our parents, but without them we are not born. Let us fight till the end. Let us fight. Thank you.'

Nagini's speech was applauded by the whole gathering as a sermon of fire which made them see the light of truth and realise their deprived position. They had decided to fight for their rightful position in the society.

*

The busy road was blocked by a train procession with banners of 'Sex Workers Union'. Each worker holding a placard conveying messages like, 'We are normal citizens', 'We may be carriers of diseases but not the originators', 'We are not immoral, you made us so', 'You get the satisfaction, but we never'. Of all the placards, one held by Kathanjali drew the attention of every onlooker and made the laughing minds ponder. The placard said, 'Who is not a prostitute?' Yes, prostitute is one who sells her body for money. A person is not body alone 'cos the dead too have a body but a decaying one, of course. The living body without self never makes a person. If a prostitute who sells her mere body is excommunicated, what of those who mortgage themselves by visiting them. What do we call those who mortgage their virtues, talents, honour of their position, and knowledge to gratify their carnal desires? A prostitute never does the job for her self-gratification but for self-existence. Yes, indeed, who is not a prostitute?

A professor who awards marks to an unworthy student… A person who promotes unholy thing in a holy place to save his life… A politician who encourages chaos for his survival… A doctor who gives fake certificate for a handful of currency notes… An engineer who communes with corrupt builder to build a defective building, thus piling up deposits… The so-called Swamis and Babas who by their tantras and mantras build strong faith in people on 'false' Gods for their survival… Unfaithful husbands and deceptive wives… Who are all these called as…? Yes, who is not a prostitute?

As the procession reached the office of the District Magistrate to submit memorandum, they were denied entrance on the pretext that he was busy in a meeting with social workers. Keerthi, a youthful woman, came and stood among them in all her grace and addressed them. The way she spoke soothed the painful hearts. The assurance she gave that she would be with them and rehabilitate them from their mire they were dwelling in confused the strained souls. More than that they were comforted by the way she behaved and in the manner she shook hands relieved them of tedious lives for a while. Katha unconsciously thought of her daughter, the only delight of her heart. She wished her daughter to be like that woman who was comforting and assuring a fresh and dignified life to the worn out souls.

*

Kathanjali's life had become tasteless and colourless. She never had time to think about her daughter. She sent the tips she was given through mail order, writing 'with love – unknown'. The desire to meet her husband was no more visible, though at random, it pricked her heart. She only hoped for her daughter but was unable to meet her. She still imagined her as a graceful young lass with her sweet looks. 'How plump were her cheeks… her childhood pranks,' she thought. All the sweet memories left by her daughter. She had been wounding her body to earn praise for her, forsaking cigar burns, filthy names and brutal behaviour.

She made up her mind to visit her daughter. She could not face her, not even in the town. Her daughter would have known of her deception and thought she must have been a party to it. She left for the place incognito and looked at all the schoolgirls, trying to find her daughter. She pointed and guessed, but failed.

She called one of the girls and inquired. 'Do you know a girl named by Prathiksha.'

'Prathiksha? There she stands… speaking to Madam.'

'Oh! You mean the girl in that satin skirt and lace overcoat?'

She hurried to meet her, but her state of morality restricted Katha. She inquired of many others for her daughter and everyone remarked in an applauding manner. 'Oh! She is a genius. She is very studious.' All these filled her heart and made it fly with joy.

Katha returned to Reyepuram on the same day and indulged herself in routine whirl.

*

She was loitering on the pavement like a lame duck on the barren canal, whose plumes were withered and body soiled with a shame of torn nakedness. Smiling at herself she was walking when suddenly she turned back beckoning to a porter's call, smiled and reciprocated to the porter denouncing her as filth. The very smile that lured many men, now plundered and stinking, is turning away the faces. The visage that built the victorious now shattered with disgust. She was a bud with all its aroma spread around, satisfying many a carnal mind, giving all she had on a beauty spread for a tiny slice of bread in return.

'She is a...' they yelled, but without knowledge of each other they queued for this dame with heir stitched ones. Recalling the words they said, she led them into her thatched shelter, standing bare for no matter the money they care. That's how ended the fare everyday.

'Hmmm... It's normal. Quite easy. Only sleeplessness resulted in hopelessness,' Katha thought.

'Hey! Are you free?' said a voice behind her. She turned with a frustrated fear of camouflaged cheer.

'Hmmm...?'

'There's a guy waiting with pockets full. Go and try.'

'Why don't you?'

'I am engaged. Moreover the drunken monk last night wounded me. I cannot...'

'Where is he?'

'Standing by the drain to drain himself.'

She stood up with a pain in her ankle, limping forward, adjusting her garment, checking her eyeliner, painting her lips and gently reached the place with a mask of gayness.

'Balu, seems there's a guy waiting here.'

'Lot many sister,' replied the cool lad.

Balu, who is not aware of his birth and infancy reared his childhood by the railway track, a conglomeration of varied lives. Who either dreams of future or curses the past save the 'present moment'. Fed on crumbs and leftovers, always stomach full and that's how the life he rules. Balu, a boy of sweet sixteen turned the hottest of life, curses the place he dwells in and wants to come out of the life he leads. Always sits by the drain which passes through their dwelling, never feels the stink of it 'cos the filth of their lives is worse than that.

'Balu, Ksheera informed me there's a man standing by the drain with an anxious look.'

'Yea! A man stood here foe a long time. Aha! I remember. Seems he is a new one. I noticed from his trembling feet and choked voice.'

'Ha, ha, ha. You know sister, he came. He looked like a gentleman… strolled over here, turned around, stood for some time. Poor man, seems a desperate soul… his body shivered… ha ha… ha…'

'Leave alone Balu, where is he?'

'You know what I want to do? Though I wished to try. What to eat, nothing left. That rascal snatched away ten for his smoke.'

'Balu, do you have anything? I like to smoke.'

'Sister, you smoke too much, that is bad for your health.' She rolled with laughter.

'Ha ha ha! Health… wealth, what sweet sounding words. Oh Balu, you really keep me in a fix of my health. Eh… There goes Nagini. Let's ask her.'

'Nagini! Oh, Nagini. Are you healthy?'

'Huh? What? What did you say? Health? …Aha. I am filth.'

Nagini's association with Reyepuram dates back to many long years. At thirteen she was orphaned and deserted by her only stepbrother. Wandering on highway she was caught and brought to this dungeon. Dungeon, she felt at the start. So what, many to talk and wish at every cross. Soon Reyepuram and Nagini became synonymous. She had a band of her own to follow and all the fresh incumbents are at her beck and call. She is now twenty with a lengthy experience having tasted the bitter fruit. All these years the life had become sweeter of it. She commands the attention of many and many are attracted towards her.

'Nagini. Where are you going now?'

'Ksheera asked me to meet her. She is leaving with Musali today.'

'Oh! Musali is hosting a feast. Then follows the fast,' exclaimed Balu.

'Leave it! Nagini, what is the cause for the feast?'

'What to say, my dear girl. She feels as if she is relaxed for the whole year. She is jumping with joy and she can't restrain herself from conveying this message to one and all she comes across.'

*

Kathanjali, lying on the bench, looked up and saw darkness of the night. She wished to hover among the infinite path so milky. She was taken aback by a though flashed her mind, reminding her harsh present. Her wounded body teased her, she asked herself whether she is the cause of her disease and other position. She never knew of it before... She ate food gathered by the pissing alley... Collected thrown leftovers in garbage pit, not with a wish to eat but she wants to live for honey, the delight of her eyes... She concealed that stupid butler's theft from her godmother, Madam Joy, not to wish a share but to protect her daughter's self respect... She had never had a desire to satisfy her urge... oh never even thought of it... but to support her daughter in disguise. She wounded her body and was prone to injury by one of the man that shot into her... 'If I never had a bond so strong. Oh no... no.'

The world is so big. Why is there no one to spare my... at least my honey. Oh... she might have forgotten me long time back. If I go and meet her, I am nothing for her. Prathiksha will never be like that... never... I wished from the stars when she was born that she should be always good. My longing for her makes me feel so strong that she should be best of all.

Her thoughts were disturbed when an urchin dragged a sack and threw it on her head. He laughed widely. 'You filthy whore! You need a pillow for that muddy head,' saying so he ran away.

World
So big and wide
Serene
All around
Stink
Anywhere we found.

She couldn't rise from her bed, rolled in bed for many hours. She took all her energy stepped on floor, fainted after she paced a few steps.

'Katha! Eh, Katha! Inspector Razack wants you... quick...' yelled Nagini from outside. Hearing no response, she came in, nursed Katha and asked her to take rest.

'Aching back, strained legs, headache... Oh, my God! I can't bear this. What's all this Nagini?'

'Oh, don't worry. You have complained of irregular periods... it is all because of that. God is very partial, you know.'

Katha visited hospital and returned to Reyepuram, where she was received with piteous looks, sympathetic smiles, pat on back as mark of comfort and cold handshakes. When she reached her hut, she was taken aback to find her baggage packed with her few dresses and the vanity wallet out. She was thrown out of Reyepuram as one would throw an expired drug. It's because of the disease... not just the disease, it was something more than that.

## Chapter Seven

# Manifestation

She walked towards the railway platform, her maiden home. Confronted with thoughts, she sat on a bench, and spent many hours in nostalgia. 'Am I responsible for my own fate. I didn't join the group for my pleasure, never had the desire to fulfil the demand of flesh. I thought of living not for my sake. No one accepted me. Everyone rejected me. Those happy years with Madam Joy ended in ash. Is it because of my deception that my days are numbered? Let me see Prathiksha for one last time. No …no. If she also rejects me… oh… no let me die in peace. Let me die in peace.' She paced a while on the platform, sat on the bench nearby, looked around and found the station almost free of crowd, a few passengers were waiting for a delayed train. They were tired of waiting and cursed Indian Railways with their heart, forgetting that they too are a part of the system. Of them, a youth in twenties had been strolling on the platform unmindful of the mismanagement of railways. He lost himself in a different world, observing people he came across, for he finds something interesting in varied mannerisms and attitudes of different people. Successful, happily married couple maintaining a distance while they walk, an unconscious dame consciously adjusting her garment, an unproven youth trying his best to imitate a favourite cine actor, snoring gentleman, nagging wife and a timid husband. Things like these amused him much. He rages with anger at one moment and becomes as cool as a cucumber, the next.

As he strolled, his eyes fell on Kathanjali, who was pale and frail with a much torn saree wrapped around, swollen legs out of dropsy, mumps on her neck and lower jaw, shaggy limbs, injured nose… carrying a cloth bag with a bunch of clothes in it. He stared at her for a while and approached her to observe her from a close distance.

Kathanjali looked at him with equal interest as she mistook him as a person eager to fulfil his urge. She was taken aback by her thought and cursed herself. As she realised how her real state of her body looks, tears rolled on her cheeks in pain and anger.

Beauty may win
Many hearts
As it blooms
Beauty may distance
Many souls
As it fades.

He went and sat beside her and offered a piece from the chocolate he was having. She looked at him in awe and smiled at his treat with thanks and hearty gratitude. The way she thanked him surprised the young man as he found precious gem of intellect in that soiled woman. He looked at her in admiration as he no longer found a stray character, which appeared outwardly a firm mind of wisdom locked up inside. He longed to know more about her. He offered her bread and coffee from a nearby cafeteria.

The young man's behaviour confused the onlookers, of which he didn't care a bit. She had the treat heartily and told him that she will never forget him in the short span of life she was going to live. She revealed her past and her longing to see her husband… but more than that, her desire and dream to see the delight of her heart, Prathiksha, her only daughter, as a virtuous woman, secured from the evils of society.

She told him that she never knew the parents who gave birth to her. She was taken from an orphanage at the age of four by a generous gentleman who spent his little income on charity all through his life. He was so affectionate to her that she was able to find in him the love of both a father and a mother. Though, his wife never treated her as a human being. Poor woman, she never knew that Kathanjali was born out of her own lust in her husband's absentia, and was discarded by that illicit woman in the orphanage by giving a false statement that she found the girl in a garbage pit.

The young man was so touched by her life that he mused for a while at the bitterness of life.

Life is a wonder
For who experience
Life is a fantasy
For who dream
Life is truth
For who discover
But life is a teacher
For who communes with life.

He realised that the time he spent on this earth is not a life for he never communed with it. His desire to know more and more from her grew and he invited her to sit by side his side. A well-dressed man who shared the bench, surprised by this young man's advances vacated the bench in disgust spitting on the platform.

Kathanjali was grateful to that youth and confessed all her past. She was very happy in her loneliness and betrayal of the so-called near and dear ones, on the pretext she was diseased and a stray character but she found bliss in isolation and loneliness. 'Loneliness is painful and depressing when you feel that you are isolated. Loneliness is a joy when you feel that you are not lifeless but a life-observing and life-giving spirit. It is a chance to observe people and to extract the essence from them,' she said. She was betrayed. 'Temptation is a bait to betray a person. The sweeter the bait the more effective is the betrayal, so that it will never appear as a betrayal.'

The young man seemed to be a bit confused with Katha's philosophical note asked her whether she was ever touched by the goodness of a gentleman. Katha rolled in laughter, walked to a water tap nearby, filled her glass with water and drank it. She stood still for a while, strolled on the platform, looked up at the sky and returned to that young man. He was shocked to see her weeping face and tried his best to control her.

The sensitive young man felt sorry that he disturbed her. The very word goodness made her recollect the very short but a long experience with the leper. After she was relieved of her burden, she told him that she laughed at the word goodness of a gentleman. The world never recognised him as a man or even a human being at least. It called him a leper or a beggar: a disease that enveloped him without his knowledge. The world considered him to be unworthy of life, but he gave life to dying Kathanjali on road when the worldly gentlemen rejected her.

Briefing all her past, Katha patted on the back of the young man unconsciously and said, 'My dear, you can't diagnose the disease of the heart and measure a person's character.'

Assemblage of limbs
Sheath of grave
Makes a human body
Woven threads dyed in hues
Makes a garment.

We cover the body naked
With a garment of out taste
To make the body appear
As we wish.

But to cover
Nakedness of heart and diseased mind
How thicker the garment
Proves transparent.

'So live the life of pure heart and adorn your mind with truth 'cos the beauty lies in the naked truth as hypocrisy lies in a camouflaged truth.'

The young man smiled at her as a token of gratitude for her advice. He resolved and wished to cherish her memory all through his life. When he looked into her eyes, he found an anxiety, which expressed something unfulfilled. She was very much aware that she was on the verge of death and her sharp knife of life had to take rest in the grave of sheath.

He asked her whether she had any promises to be kept or desires to be fulfilled at her last stage of life. The sensitive youth trembled as he uttered the last words 'last stage'. He asked her to excuse him for he was plain in making a statement about her being on the last stage. Katha smiled at him in pity and was silent for a few moments. She said that she had a longing to see her daughter. Her heart beats for her. She breathes air, begs for food, is patient at people's curses to survive, to live life with not a desire to live long in this stinking world, but to see her daughter grown up.

The young man, out of ignorance thought she could not afford a journey to the place where her daughter stays. He took a few currency notes and tried to offer Katha. He asked her to make the journey and fulfil her desire.

Katha smiled with thanks and said that she never had a desire to see her daughter grown 'big'. She never dreamt of the physical beauty of her 'honey' Prathiksha, for she considers mortal beauty as ash. She longed to see her daughter with a mature mind enveloped with beauty of goodness. She longs to see virtuous, firm heart of her daughter, who exists in this ill-mannered world. She longs to see the lesson of charity taught by good grandpa, the leper, reflected in her daughter. She longs to see her daughter as a resolved spirit to stay away from sin. She longs to see her as one who measures people in truth… Kathanjali was silent for a while and the young man could not say a word. But he had aroused the truthful character in Kathanjali, which yearned for truth in her daughter.

He lost himself in deep thought of Katha's philosophy, a longing for truth and goodness, desire to see them adorned by her daughter, and which would make a beautiful Prathiksha. His youthful heart dreamt of the fellowship with that unknown girl of goodness and he desired to see her. He said to himself,

'It is a bliss
To see the girl
Who is good

It is treasure
To meet the girl
Who is beauty

For that good girl
Is beautiful
No, no, no…
Beauty self she is
As the goodness is she.'

The dreaming young man was disturbed by an announcement of the train's arrival. He left Katha wishing her goodbye.

The train halted with a sound of horn in lower tempo as if heaving a sigh of relief from the burden of the passengers of complex cultures with complicated minds. People who came to receive their kith and kin rushed in all the directions to find them. Some with a hearty gesture of welcome, while others with Monalisa-masked faces cursing the arrival of their guests. Vendors of tea and snacks had their business to the core and the newspaper boys walking on the platform convincing them to buy, wishing in their heart for they could find only readers but not buyers. All these incidents at the early hours of the day made the railway station wear a festive look.

Katha watched the things that took place and rendezvous of the people pierced her heart with envy. She looked at every youthful girl and imagined Prathiksha in that image.

The very thoughts of Prathiksha increased her urge to meet her and she resolved to see her daughter anyhow. She took her cloth bag and moved forward towards the train halted at the other platform. 'It is about to start in an hour,' she said to herself. While she climbed up the steps of the bridge, which connected the two platforms, she thought of the ticket for the journey.

'Oh! No one will ask me. They will think that I am a beggar. Or if I have to I'll hide in the toilet or move from one compartment to another. That's what many rich people do. That day, when I visited Prathiksha last time, a gentleman in a costly suit, who was travelling without ticket, offered a ten rupee note to that Ticket Inspector and had a sleeper berth easily. Of course there was much room vacant at that time... No one will question me because of my appearance.'

She tried to convince herself to travel ticketless. She collected many incidents of corruption she had witnessed in trains. Hence she did not find anything wrong in travelling without paying.

'Oh, but that's an act of deception and only a deceiver commits it... If I travel ticketless to see my grown up daughter with good and uprightness, I am making a fool of myself expecting other offenders to be right. She is my daughter. What she will learn from me? Am I worthy of being a mother? All these days I affirmed myself that I am not a prostitute. If I sell my virtue now in a fifty rupees note, I am... yes, I am a prostitute... no use in feeling bad about the world, the profession I was in.

'Oh, God! What shall I do? I have only this amount... a fifty rupees note... I thought of sending this amount to Prathiksha. If I buy a ticket, I'll have nothing to give her. No, no, anyone can give money, but not virtue. I'll go and meet Prathiksha and disclose that unknown in me and say why I could not send money to her. Hope she'll understand and learn the virtue of righteousness. If she learns this virtue, I would feel like a millionaire who passed all his property to his daughter. But will she understand that... yes... she'll understand. My daughter is a good girl. She may be very young in age but she is very mature otherwise. Other day I gave a lecture to a couple, whom I came across in a train, on virtue of marriage. If a husband and a wife lack understanding and love and if they do not respect each other, it is not a marriage at all, but a perfect adultery. I asked the woman to be righteous at every moment of her life and now I am travelling ticketless...

'I curse corrupt ticket collectors and deceiving passengers. Who am I if I travel ticketless? But the money is for Prathiksha... OK, I'll give her money, this fifty rupees note and she will know the way I made the journey. My daughter of goodness may despise me throughout her life... better than my longing of all these years... Oh God, but is it better to die without meeting than be despised for good at the cost of fifty rupees... OK, I'll go and buy the ticket and travel in a royal way.'

Katha's conflict of truthfulness and deception was disturbed with blaring slogans made by a group of students, as they appeared to be, at the entrance of railway station. She observed every participant of the rally and traced an ingredient of hypocrisy, flavoured with verbal justification to demand justice. They were taking out the rally to the state capital, the banner indicated. The angry protestors threw stones at the station master's office, ticket counters and at other places, not caring for the direction nor the result.

The rally moved on the platform in an angry note, demanding justice and in the process stampeding people. The unjustified mob that never practised justice was ignorant of justice as a quality, so they demanded justice quantitatively.

Katha too was injured in the violence and bled a lot of blood from the little she had in her body.

Corruption and chaos
Enveloped the world
Justice and rule
Interpreted to one's convenience
Protests and strikes
To fulfil one's demands
Rule of law is the golden rule
Of the humanity – they preach
Love the country
Philosophy, every one teach

People are the nations
We forget and divide and fight
Never care for hungry souls
While we fight to end in hunger.

Continuously haunted by death, she took all energy to walk and buy a ticket. She looked around the station, a home for the homeless and an undisturbed shelter for the deserted.

Coffee shops, paper boys, porters, dustbins, cement benches, things of life and lifeless alike were her company all those days. She never hoped that she would see them again. She wept as she departed, as if she left her father's home.

Katha lay on a bench without any food, had only a sip of coffee, then boarded the train and left to see her dear daughter Prathiksha. By the time she reached her destination, she was damn tired.

*

People wondered at the weakling figure, pale face, wrinkled cheeks, shabby clothes, sagging limbs. Everyone gave way to her. Now she had to face Prathiksha. She walked by, the canal fish dried up on the bank, miracles with bamboo sticks, crossed the bridge. She walked through the labyrinth, tired, strained… Oh, God… She fainted.

Diseased Katha slowly opened her eyes and found herself in the lap of a young dame holding a glass of some kind of mineral fluid and nursing her. She was surrounded by a group of girls looking at her.

'Oh, dear one. Leave me alone. Do not touch me. Let not the sin pass over to you.'

'Oh! No… no… Do not speak nonsense, nothing passes through with a touch… We are not magnets… We are human beings,' saying so she took her into her lap and poured the energy drink into her mouth.

'Thanks a lot, dear one… You are a very good girl… I always wish the same for my dear girl, the delight of my heart… May I know your name young lass?'

'People call me Prathiksha.'

'Pra…thi…ksha…' Tears rolled in mirth of meeting… for it was the only hope of her life… at last fulfilled.

And Prathiksha felt Katha's head heavy.

Journey of the 'unknown' is known

And ends here.

The mortal of Kathanjali lay in a passive state. People around realised her as the one who worked for charity home and was the confidante of Madam Joy.

Madam Joy rushed to the place and took the mortal to her quarters, the place where the now dead soul lived in peace and bliss with her spiritual mother. The workers, inmates, including the regretful butler were present on that occasion. The dead body made these people recollect their relationship with Kathanjali and her goodness.

The daughter, who realised the 'unknown', was comforted by everyone present. Prathiksha could not see the diseased, soiled Kathanjali, but a loving mother with beauty in truth.